Katie

cupcakes and wedding bells

SIMON SPOTLIGHT

An imprint of Simon & Schuster Children's Publishing Division

1230 Avenue of the Americas, New York, New York 10020

First Simon Spotlight paperback edition May 2020

Copyright © 2020 by Simon & Schuster, Inc.

All rights reserved, including the right of reproduction
in whole or in part in any form.

SIMON SPOTLIGHT and colophon are registered trademarks of
Simon & Schuster, Inc.

Text by Tracey West

Chapter header illustrations by Daniel Tornow

Designed by Laura Roode

For information about special discounts for bulk purchases, please contact
Simon & Schuster Special Sales at 1-866-506-1949
or business@simonandschuster.com.

Manufactured in the United States of America 0320 OFF

2 4 6 8 10 9 7 5 3 1

ISBN 978-1-5344-6538-1 (hc)

ISBN 978-1-5344-6537-4 (pbk)

ISBN 978-1-5344-6539-8 (eBook)

Library of Congress Control Number 2020930734

CUPCAKE DIARIES

Katie

cupcakes
and
wedding
bells

by coco simon

Simon Spotlight

New York   London   Toronto   Sydney   New Delhi

CHAPTER 1

Saturday Morning

$\mathcal{H}$ow are those macarons coming, Katie?" Melissa asked me.

I gently touched the top of one of the pale orange, circular cookies with the top of my finger. Teeny dots of the cookie stuck to my finger.

"No skin yet," Melissa replied. The pastry chef's cheeks were flushed red, and strands of her brown hair were spilling out from under her white bandana. "It's this humidity. How can it be so humid already? It's only May!"

"I don't know," I said. "It's not even Memorial Day, but it feels like summer."

My own brown hair was pulled back into a ponytail, which was doing a decent job of keeping me cool. But Melissa was right. It was unusually sticky in the Chez Daniel kitchen that Saturday morning.

"How's that lemon curd coming?" Melissa asked.

"I was just about to put it in the blast chiller," I told her. She walked up and dipped a spoon into the pot. Then she tasted it. "Nice! Not too sweet, and not too tart."

"Thanks," I said, and I could feel my cheeks flush but not from the heat—but from pride.

I'd been working in the kitchen of Chez Daniel, a fancy restaurant near my town. The place is owned by my Dessert Dad, Marc Daniel Brown, which is how I got the gig. I call him my Dessert Dad because he wasn't here for the first courses of my life. He divorced my mom when I was a baby and went off to become a chef. Recently, he'd been trying to make up for lost time, and since he knew I loved to bake, he offered me an internship at the restaurant, helping Melissa.

Once I figured out that Marc Daniel Brown was my Dessert Dad and would never be a real dad to me, working at his restaurant became a lot easier. It was an amazing experience.

"What can I do now?" I asked Melissa.

"I've got ten pounds of strawberries that need

to be hulled," she replied. "They're in the cooler."

"Great," I said. "I should be able to finish that before Jeff picks me up."

I went to grab the strawberries from the cooler and bumped into Dessert Dad on the way in.

"Hey, Katie," he said. "What's on the menu today?"

"A trio of macarons with vanilla ice cream, and strawberry mousse with shortbread cookies," I replied. "I made the cookies myself."

"Great, I can't wait to try some," he said. "Hey, Cecile has been begging me to bring you bowling with us again. Are you free on Tuesday after school?"

Tuesday was the one day during the week that the restaurant was closed, and the day Dessert Dad liked to do things with his daughters—me and my three little half-sisters, Cecile, Ella, and Riley.

"I have to check my schedule," I told him. "Things have been kind of crazy lately, with the . . ."

I didn't finish my sentence. Dessert Dad knew what I meant. My mom—his ex-wife—was marrying Jeff in a few months. I knew Dessert Dad was happy with his wife, Jasmine, but still, it felt weird talking about Mom's wedding with him.

"Sure. Text me," he said.

"I will," I promised, and I piled the quarts of

fresh strawberries onto a metal pan and carried them back to the pastry prep area.

I managed to do all the strawberries, plus finish the orange-lemon macarons, before it was time for me to go at noon.

"Thanks, Katie," Melissa said as I hung up my apron. "Going to a Cupcake meeting?"

"Yeah, we've got to plan the cupcakes for the wedding," I told her. Talking about the wedding with Melissa wasn't weird at all.

"That sounds like fun," she said. "Let me know if you need any pointers. I used to work for a wedding caterer. Weddings are so much fun!"

"Thanks! I'll let everybody know," I said.

Then I stepped outside into the May sunshine. My soon-to-be stepdad, Jeff, was parked in the back of the restaurant. My soon-to-be stepsister, Emily, was in the back seat. I slid in next to her.

"Hey, Katie," Jeff said.

"What did you make today, Katie?" Emily asked, her dark eyes shining.

I told her about every item on the dessert menu in detail. She's in sixth grade, and she's pretty cool. At first I thought we were nothing alike. She's superneat and clean, and she likes to eat healthy food like salad most of the time. But since Mom

4

and Jeff started dating, Emily and I started to spend more time together, and she was very curious about the Cupcake Club. Now she's kind of an honorary member who helps us out sometimes.

"That strawberry mousse sounds amazing," Emily said.

"And good job on making those cookies all by yourself," Jeff said.

I shrugged. "They're just shortbread cookies. Pretty easy."

"Yes, but they're being served in a top-rated restaurant," Jeff said. "That's something special, Katie."

I looked over to see Emily smiling at me, which was kind of a relief. A lot of things can go wrong when you take two families and stick them together. Emily could have gotten jealous when Jeff was nice to me, or I could get jealous when Mom did something nice for Emily. But luckily, things weren't like that with us.

In fact, ever since Jeff had proposed to Mom, we'd starting acting like a family. We went to Vinnie's Pizza every other Friday, when Jeff had Emily, and got our "usual" order: two veggie pizzas, salad, garlic knots, and chicken fingers. When we went to the movies together, we all shared a jumbo popcorn. We all loved running, and we had a special trail through the park that we'd dubbed the Green-Brown Trail—because Jeff and Emily's last name is Green, and Mom and I are Browns.

Jeff pulled up in front of my friend Mia's house, where we were having an afternoon Cupcake Club meeting. Ever since I formed the club with my friends Mia, Alexis, and Emma, we've been busy "building our business," as Alexis would say. We put up flyers and handed out business cards, and now we have a baking job every week. That all takes a lot of planning, and we often do it during school at lunch or in our free time at one another's houses. That day we were planning for something really special to me: Mom and Jeff's wedding. It was special to Emily, too, and she was coming to the meeting.

"When should I pick you girls up?" Jeff asked.

"Around four," I replied as Emily and I got out of the car.

We said good-bye to Jeff and walked up to Mia's front door. It opened before we could ring the bell.

"Yay, you're here!" Mia said, and her teeny white dogs, Tiki and Milkshake, yapped at our feet with excitement.

Emily knelt down to pet the dogs. "They're so cute!"

"Cute and loud," Mia said. "Tiki! Milkshake! Quiet down!"

The dogs obeyed, and we followed Mia into the house. I heard the sounds of roaring car motors and squealing brakes and traced it to the video game being played in the living room by her stepbrother, Dan, and cousin Sebastian.

"Can you *please* turn that down?" Mia yelled. "We're trying to have a Cupcake meeting."

The boys paused the game. "We'll do anything you say if you give us cupcakes," Sebastian said with a grin.

"We're not baking today," Mia told him.

"No deal then!" Dan cried, and they continued their game.

Mia rolled her eyes at Emily and me. "Sorry. You would think *I* was the oldest one in this family," she said.

She led us into the dining room, where Emma was scrolling on a laptop and Alexis was opening up giant spreadsheets on the table. She'd pulled her wavy red hair into a ponytail away from her face and looked ready for business.

"Wow, this looks like you're planning some kind of military operation," I remarked, sitting down at the table.

"A wedding is like a military operation," Alexis replied. "Everything has to be planned out to the minute, and if one thing goes wrong, the whole thing collapses."

"Isn't that exaggerating a little bit, Alexis?" Mia asked.

Alexis looked at her. "Even if I am, why take a chance? The Brown-Green wedding needs to be perfect!"

After Mom and Jeff had decided that they wanted cupcakes at their wedding instead of cake, they'd asked the Cupcake Club to make them. The club had said yes, of course, and then Alexis had volunteered to help organize the wedding.

I think it will be fun to plan a wedding, Alexis had said. *Besides, it will look amazing on a college application!*

Mom had agreed because she knows there's nobody more organized and professional in Maple Grove than Alexis.

I leaned over to look at her spreadsheets.

"Which one of these is for the cupcakes?" I asked.

Alexis tapped one. "I began by listing all the things we need to figure out. How many cupcakes do we need to bake? How will we display them?

8

Do we need a special cupcake for the bride and groom? How long will it take to bake and decorate? Whose kitchen will we use?"

"Does it say anything about what flavors they're going to be?" I asked. In my mind, that was the most important thing. I'm not great at decorating cupcakes—Mia and Emma are best at that—but as long as a cupcake tastes amazing, I don't care what it looks like.

"Yes, there's a chart here," Alexis said. "And Emma has been researching wedding cupcake trends."

Emma, who had been quiet up until now, looked up from her laptop.

"Sorry, the images are so beautiful that I think they hypnotized me," she said. "These cupcakes look like works of art!"

Emma turned her laptop to face us, and we saw a collage of images of beautiful cupcakes arranged on towers to mimic the shape of a tall, stacked wedding cake. Close-ups of the cupcakes showed smooth white icing, some carefully decorated with piped rosettes, and others with gold, silver, or rose-gold pearls.

"Those are so pretty!" Emily said. "They look like something from a fairy-tale wedding. Can we make ones that look just like these?" She pointed to a tower of white iced cupcakes decorated with pink icing flowers.

Mia spoke up. "First we need to know the wedding colors—like what color dresses everyone will be wearing, and what color flowers will be on the tables. Do we know that?"

"I've been asking Mrs. Brown, but she hasn't decided yet," Alexis said. She looked at me. "Can you get her to decide, Katie?"

"I can ask her," I replied. "I've been mostly thinking about cupcake flavors. Mom and I don't talk about wedding details too much. I don't even know what dress I'm wearing."

"Me either," Emily said.

Alexis shook her head. "Well, if I were you, I wouldn't wait too much longer to figure it out," she said. "Your mom told me the head count for the wedding is around a hundred and ten. That's a lot of cupcakes to make. And that takes planning, too. We want everything to be perfect. "

I was starting to feel anxious. "Can we talk about flavors now?" I asked. That was something I could control. "I was thinking maybe we do cupcakes with one of Mom and Jeff's favorite flavors. Like, they both love gingerbread."

"That's a good idea, but gingerbread kind of feels like winter, doesn't it? And this is a fall wedding," Emma pointed out.

Mom and Jeff didn't have a date yet, but they were thinking of getting married in October because they loved the fall.

I took out my phone and scrolled through the list I had made. "Okay, what about apple? They both love apple pie."

Emma's blue eyes lit up. "Ooh, apple cupcakes with brown sugar icing! That feels very fall-like."

Then Emily chimed in. "I know! They both like Earl Grey tea, right, Katie?" she asked. "I looked it up, and there are lots of cupcake recipes based on tea flavors."

Emma started typing on her laptop. "You're right, Emily. And we could do a white vanilla icing with pretty decorations."

"That does sound yummy," I said, wishing I had thought of it.

"But we have to remember," Alexis said, "not everyone likes Earl Grey tea. One of the most popular wedding cake flavors is vanilla with strawberry filling. Maybe we need to do something basic, so everyone will enjoy it."

"Basic and boring," Mia said. "I think we need

11

to know the colors of the wedding before we can decide on a flavor. Because if they're pink, then the apple pie ones might not work."

"I don't think Mom would pick pink," I said. "But I'm not sure. I promise to ask Mom."

"We should do test batches of some of the flavors soon," Alexis suggested. "And even if we don't use them for Katie's mom's wedding, we could offer them to our clients. They're always looking for something new."

"We can bake at my house," I offered. "But we have plenty of time, right?"

Alexis frowned. "Most weddings are planned a year in advance. We don't even have half that time. We should do a test session as soon as possible."

"Maybe we should bake somewhere else, and that way we could surprise your Mom and Mr. Green," Emma said.

I shrugged. "Sure. Whatever you think."

"In the meantime, we've got to make a plan for the two dozen chocolate cupcakes we need for that birthday next week," Alexis said.

Then we launched into our regular meeting, but my head wasn't in it. Suddenly, I felt panicked.

My mom's wedding was happening in five months. We didn't have wedding colors, I didn't have a dress, and the Cupcake Club had to figure out how to make more than one hundred gorgeous cupcakes that everyone would love to eat.

Even with Alexis organizing things, it seemed like an impossible challenge!

CHAPTER 2

Change Is Good ... Isn't It?

The volleyball sailed over the net and then over Mia's head in front of me.

"You can do it, Silly Arms!" my friend George called from beside me.

I jumped up and thrashed around wildly, hoping to make contact with the ball. I didn't. I missed it completely, and it bounced on the floor next to me.

"Our point!" Eddie Rossi called out from across the net.

"Better luck next time, Silly Arms," George said.

Thankfully, there wasn't a next time because Ms. Goodman blew her whistle and told us that gym class was over. I gratefully jogged to the locker room and changed out of my official Park Street Middle School gym uniform and back into my jeans and one of my favorite T-shirts that read STAY CALM AND BAKE ON.

When I emerged from the locker room, I ran up to George.

"You know, just because I have silly arms doesn't mean you have to call me Silly Arms," I said, but not in a hurt way. George started calling me that at the start of middle school because I look like one of those sprinklers with the arms that wave around wildly. It was a joke between us, and it had led to us becoming good friends.

"One of these days, your hands will make contact with a volleyball," George replied. "And then maybe I'll stop."

We fell into step with each other and started walking to the cafeteria.

"I'll stick to running," I said. "I don't know why they make us do gym, anyway. I mean, not everybody's good at everything. I read somewhere where kids could get credit for gym by shoveling snow for the elderly or cleaning up trash in parks. That makes a lot more sense than forcing us to play volleyball and dodgeball."

"I'd rather play volleyball than shovel snow," George replied.

I shrugged. "Not me," I said.

"So, do you want to play basketball at the park this weekend? Or would you rather rake some leaves or dig a ditch?" George teased.

"I'll stick to basketball, thanks, but I'm not sure if I can," I replied. "Mom and Jeff's wedding is coming up in a few months, and the Cupcake Club is making the cupcakes, and I think we need to meet this weekend because we don't even have the flavor picked out yet. And I think we also have a gig, but I'm not sure because my mind's been so busy thinking about the wedding, and—"

"Okay," George interrupted. He seemed bummed.

"I'm really sorry," I said. "I just have to check and see what the Cupcake Club is doing. Life has been so crazy with—"

"Yeah, I got it," George said abruptly.

We walked the rest of the way to the cafeteria without talking. That was unusual because both George and I like to talk. A lot. Then it hit me: Maybe George was tired of hearing about my mom marrying his math teacher. The more I thought about it, the more I realized that he clammed up whenever the wedding came up.

I must be boring him to death! I thought, and I started to ask about it, but the bell rang. He gave me a nod and jogged off to meet up with his friends.

I headed to the table where I had sat with Mia, Emma, and Alexis since the beginning of middle school—it's where we all met. A P–B–and–J cupcake my mom had sent with me for lunch had given us all something to talk about and led us to forming the Cupcake Club.

I got there first, and Mia and Alexis showed up next and opened their lunch bags. Emma came up with a school lunch tray holding a plate with some kind of meat patty, sad-looking green beans, and mashed potatoes.

"Mystery meat day," she joked, and she took a seat at the table. "I meant to make my lunch last night, but I got home late from my shoot. And then I had to do my math worksheet, and I totally forgot."

Have I mentioned yet that Emma is a model? She's got long, blond hair and a perfect smile, so I wasn't surprised when she got asked to model dresses for a local clothing boutique. She's not famous or anything, but she's been getting more and more gigs. She models for catalogs and newspaper ads and stuff like that. I always thought modeling would be an easy job. Just stand there and look pretty, right? It's a lot harder than it looks. One time I went with Emma to one of her casting calls for a magazine ad. I just went to keep her company. It turned out some people thought I had an interesting look, and they offered *me* the modeling job. It was one of the hardest things I've ever done. *You* try wearing a heavy winter coat on a hot summer day for a photograph and try to look like you're having a good time! And the more people told me to *just relax and have fun*, the more nervous I got. And it showed in the photographs. No matter how hard I tried, I looked awkward and uncomfortable. Emma, meanwhile, is a natural. She can look straight into the camera and look like it's the happiest day of her life, even if she can't wait for it to be over. That day was "one and done" for me. I never wanted to model again after that, and I admire Emma even more for the great job she always does.

Alexis looked over at the mystery meat on Emma's plate. "Do you want half of my sandwich?"

"No, thanks," Emma said. "The mashed potatoes are good. And if you chop the meat up into tiny pieces and mix it in, it's not so bad."

"Hey, I was just wondering what our schedule is this weekend," I said. "I mean, I know I should know, but my brain is spaghetti these days."

"Oh, Katie! Your brain is always spaghetti!" Mia said, laughing. "You *love* spaghetti."

"This is very true," I admitted. "But you know what I mean. All I can think about is the wedding."

"We've got to bake two dozen cupcakes for the Delgado birthday party at three p.m. Saturday," Alexis said, without even having to look it up. "Baking and decorating is scheduled for my house at ten a.m."

"I'll be at my dad's," Mia said.

Mia's parents are divorced, just like mine. The difference is that Mia's dad isn't a Dessert Dad, like Marc Daniel Brown. Mia has spent every other weekend with him since the divorce, and she spends a bunch of weeks with him in the summer. I guess you could say he is more like a Brunch Dad. And you get a lot more food at brunch than you do at dessert. Mia and her dad are really close.

"But you're getting me the materials for the decorations, right?" Alexis asked.

"I can drop them off tomorrow night," Mia responded.

"Great," Alexis said. "My dad said he'd bring me to the party to drop off the finished cupcakes. It's only two dozen, so I can handle the setup."

"Thanks," I said. "What about doing a test batch of some of the wedding flavors this weekend? Maybe Sunday?"

"We're going to visit my grandma," Alexis replied. "Maybe we should do it the following week, when all four of us are around?"

"Sounds good to me," I said. "I'll see if Emily can come." And I made a mental note to tell George that I could play basketball with him on Sunday.

Alexis reached into her backpack and pulled out her planner. "We should really try to get this done soon because I'm sure you'll be really busy as the wedding gets closer."

"Well, mostly busy with the cupcakes," I said. "I don't have to do much else to plan."

"But what about moving?" Alexis asked.

"What do you mean?" I replied. "We're not moving."

"You're not?" Alexis asked. "I just assumed that you were. Your house only has those two bedrooms. Will you be sharing a bedroom with Emily when she visits Mr. Green on the weekends?"

I know it sounds weird, but I had never thought this through before Alexis mentioned it. I guess it was in the back of my mind, but I'd kept it there, not wanting to think about what this marriage really meant.

"I—I don't know," I admitted. "Mom told me a while ago that Jeff and Emily would be living with us if they got married, so I don't think we're moving. I'm not sure what she was thinking about Emily. Maybe she could sleep on the couch? It's not like Emily will be living with us full-time."

"I don't think your mom and Mr. Green would want Emily to sleep on a couch," Mia said gently. "Maybe she can sleep in your room."

"You mean like a sleepover?" I asked.

"More like a roommate," Alexis said. "Maybe they'll put up bunk beds for you two."

The thought of sharing my bedroom with someone, even someone nice like Emily, made my blood run cold. I put down the string cheese I'd been about to eat. My stomach felt heavy.

Mia put her hand on my arm. "Don't worry about it, Katie. I'm sure your mom has a solution."

"Yeah," I said weakly.

"And you and your mom are so close," Emma added. "Like best friends. If you don't want to share a room with Emily, I'm sure she'd understand."

So close. The words echoed in my head. Would we still be close after she married Jeff? With Emily hanging around all the time?

I'd resented Emily when Mom and Jeff first began dating because Emily started joining in everything I did—even my basketball games with

George. I had grown to really like her, but did I want her to be my sister?

I tried to imagine Emily in the room with me, giggling and sharing secrets, but I couldn't. I am not a giggling-and-sharing-secrets kind of girl. I am a throw-my-dirty-socks-on-the-floor-and-dance-with-headphones-on kind of girl. An eat-ice-cream-in-bed-and-then-burp-really-loud kind of girl. And I couldn't do those things if I shared a space with Emily.

I suddenly got weirdly possessive of everything in my room. I imagined Emily going through my books, through my clothes, trying everything on. It was silly because Emily wasn't like that at all. She was very sweet and respectful. But still, I couldn't stop these crazy thoughts from running through my head.

Emily won't be there all the time, I thought, but then I remembered something: Jeff *would* be there all the time. Every breakfast. Every dinner. What would happen to my Friday night tradition with Mom, when we got into our pajamas and ate takeout food? Would Jeff join us in flannel pj's with math symbols all over them? Ugh!

And what about breakfast for dinner? Jeff always teased us about that tradition and said that if breakfast for dinner made sense, then people should also eat dinner for breakfast, too. And when I argued that cold pizza makes a great breakfast, he made a face. Would breakfast for dinner be forever over with?

I sat there, thoughts spinning in my head, while my friends changed the subject and talked about some teen star who does makeup tutorials. When the bell rang, I stood up, left my uneaten lunch on the table (sorry, lunch monitors!) and darted straight into the hallway.

"Katie, where's the fire?"

I had almost bumped into Jeff, my future stepdad, known as Mr. Green to the rest of the kids in my school.

"Oh, um, s-sorry," I stammered. "Just, um, late to . . . locker . . . hall . . ."

I darted away.

Mom was the one marrying Jeff, but the weird thing was that I was going to be spending more time with him than she was. I was going to see him every day at school. And every night for dinner. Boring, bland, basic dinner, perfect for a math teacher.

Tears stung my eyes, but I held them back. I had four more classes to get through. But all I wanted to do was get home—my home, with just Mom and me—and enjoy it while it lasted.

CHAPTER 3

Save the Date

On the bus ride home from school, Mia was texting her friend Ava from Manhattan while I stared out the window, biting my lip. Since lunch, I hadn't stopped worrying about how different my life was going to be once Mom married Jeff.

The bus stopped at the end of my street, and I said good-bye to Mia and hurried off. As I walked toward my house, I named all the other homes on the street in my head. There was where Mrs. Yashioka lived, the nice lady who brought us bouquets of flowers from her garden in the summer. Then there were the Pilieres, a nice young couple who'd just had the cutest baby. Then there was Jim, who worked for the gas company and helped Mom fix our front railings when they got loose. And across the street was Mrs. Bach, who crocheted me a little orange pumpkin every Halloween.

I stopped in front of my house. It was the smallest house on the block, with white shingles that were peeling here and there and flowerpots on each side of the green front door. Dandelions were starting to sprout on the front lawn, and Mom and I never tried to kill them or pull them out. We thought they were pretty.

Does Jeff think dandelions are pretty? I wondered, and I realized I didn't know. Tears started to well up in my eyes again, and after I let myself in, I dropped my backpack in the hallway, ran upstairs, and threw myself onto my bed. Then I began to sob.

How could I have forgotten all the changes that were coming? Would I ever be able to cry in my room again, or would I have Emily staring at me while I did it? What was it going to be like having Jeff around *all the time*?

"All the time!" I wailed, and then I buried my face in my pillow again.

I cried and cried until I ran out of tears. Then I grabbed one of the stuffed animals on my bed, curled up, and fell asleep.

❀

I woke to Mom shaking my shoulder. "Katie, are you okay? Are you feeling sick?"

"No," I said, sitting up.

"Didn't you see the note I left about heating up the lasagna?" she asked. "Jeff and Emily will be here for dinner soon."

Of course, I thought. But I didn't say it out loud. It was already starting. I couldn't even get in a good cry in my room without my new stepdad and stepsister interfering.

"Do you want me to heat up the lasagna now?" I asked.

"I already did it," Mom replied. "Please set the table while I make a salad. We can always eat it while we're waiting for the lasagna to be done."

Then she felt my head. "You don't feel warm. But you look flushed."

"I'm fine," I insisted, and then I jumped out of bed and did a twirl. "See?"

Mom laughed. "All right. I guess you're just starting to do that teenage thing where you sleep all the time," she said. "I hope this doesn't mean you're staying up late texting. Joanne's son was up until three in the morning last night!"

Joanne is a woman who works in my mom's dental office.

"Mom, are you really comparing me to Dean?" I asked. "He's, like, sixteen."

Mom ruffled my hair. "You'll be sixteen before I know it, Katie."

We headed downstairs to the kitchen. Our house isn't big enough for a dining room—Mom and I eat around a small wooden table that can squeeze in four people if you try hard enough. I was just finishing putting down the utensils when the doorbell rang.

"Can you get that, please?" Mom asked.

"Sure," I said, and I walked to the front door.

"Hi, Katie!" Jeff said. He held a long, skinny loaf of bread in one hand, and Emily stood in front of him.

"Hey," I said, and I turned my back on them and walked inside.

"Emily's been telling me about some of the flavors you girls have been cooking up," Jeff said behind me.

I spun around. "Emily, those ideas are secret until we're ready to present them," I said.

She looked upset. "I'm sorry, Katie. I didn't know."

I hadn't wanted to make her feel bad, so I tried to lighten things up by joking. "It's okay, Emily. Just remember, what happens in Cupcake Club stays in Cupcake Club. This is top secret stuff!"

Emily nodded solemnly. "I promise, Katie."

"Everyone, have a seat," Mom said, placing the salad bowl on the table. "The lasagna's almost done. Let's eat our salad first."

"I'll slice the bread," Jeff offered, and he opened up one of the cabinet doors to find a cutting board.

"Wrong one," I told him. "It's the one on the left."

"Thanks, Katie," he said with a big smile. I'd always appreciated Jeff's smiley nature, but right then it really bugged me. Was I going to have to deal with his smiles, even when I didn't feel like smiling?

Soon we were all sitting around the table, eating our salad and buttering our bread like one big happy family. Mom and Jeff kept staring at each other and smiling. I wanted to ignore them, but I couldn't help looking at them.

Finally Jeff nodded to Mom, and she cleared her throat.

"So . . . ," she began. "We have decided on a wedding date."

"Is it on October thirty-first?" Emily asked. "Because I saw this Halloween wedding on one of the wedding websites, and it was so cool."

Jeff shook his head. "No, actually, we've decided to tie the knot sooner than that," he said. "June twenty-sixth."

"You mean, *next* year?" I asked.

Mom shook her head. "No, like Jeff said, we want to do it sooner. This June. In about six weeks."

"Why so fast?" I blurted out.

Mom and Jeff looked at each other and started goofy smiling again.

"We just couldn't wait to get married any longer," Mom said, never losing her smile. "So we thought we'd get married right after school lets out. And then he and I will go away to a cabin in upstate New York for a few days."

"Cool! I'll stay with Mom," Emily said.

And where will I stay? I wondered. I didn't have a second parent like Emily did to take care of me when my main parent was away. I had only Dessert Dad.

I thought quickly. There was no way I could adjust to the idea of my whole new life in just *six* weeks. Maybe logic would work. Mom was a dentist. Jeff was a math teacher. They both lived for logic!

"Alexis says it takes a year to plan for a wedding,"

I said. "Six weeks has got to be impossible, right?"

"We're not planning anything fancy," Mom said. "And I'm sure if anyone can help us figure out how to make this work, Alexis can."

"But won't it be too hot in June for a wedding?" I tried.

"June is the most popular month for weddings, Katie," Mom replied. "We'll be following tradition."

"I think June is a nice month for a wedding," Emily said. She didn't seem upset by the change at all. She smiled at me happily.

Of course she didn't, I thought. She gets to have alone time with her mom whenever she wants. I'll never get alone time with my mom ever again!

"Well, you'd better call Alexis right away," I said. "She's got a ton of questions for you."

"I will. I promise!" Mom said.

Then it was time to eat the lasagna, and the conversation turned to the new sushi place opening up downtown and Emily's art class. When it was time for Jeff and Emily to leave, Mom and Jeff made a big show of kissing each other right in front of me and Emily.

"Love you," Jeff said.

"Love you, too," Mom replied, and they kissed each other again. Emily rolled her eyes at me.

Well, at least we agree on something about this relationship, I thought. *Mom and Jeff are too mushy!*

Mom stood on the steps until they drove away and then joined me in the kitchen. We both started cleaning up. My mom was so happy she started dancing around the kitchen. I had been planning to unload all my worries on her, but seeing her so happy, I just couldn't.

"You're in an awfully good mood for a Monday," I said as I loaded plates into the dishwasher.

"I'm just so excited, Katie!" she said. "I know it must seem like we're rushing the wedding, but Jeff and I are just so happy. He's so kind, Katie, and he's such a good listener. And he's always there for me when I need him."

I knew Mom was thinking of Dessert Dad when she said that—how he'd left her alone with a little helpless baby (me) and never looked back. And I couldn't argue that Jeff wasn't a good guy. He really was great. So I decided to let Mom be happy for the rest of the night.

After I washed up in the sink, she grabbed my hands.

"Katie, sit down. There's something I need to ask you," she said.

Uh-oh, I thought. *This is where she asks me to share*

31

a room with Emily. I immediately started thinking up plans that involved converting the garage into my own separate apartment. But that's not what Mom wanted to talk about.

"Katie, I would love you to be my maid of honor," Mom said.

That hit me out of nowhere. "Me? Really?"

"Who else would I ask?" Mom said, and her eyes filled with tears. "Katie, you are everything to me. There is no one in this world I would rather have by my side when I marry Jeff. Will you do it?"

"Of course!" I said, and I whooped. "Wait, does this mean I have to throw you a bachelorette party where we go into the city in a limo and wear silly matching T-shirts?"

"Please do not do anything like that," Mom said. "No, all you have to do is walk down the aisle with me."

"I can do that," I said.

"Jeff and I are going to ask Emily to be a bridesmaid," Mom said. "I want her to be a part of the ceremony too."

"Cool!" I said. "Wait, we'll need dresses, right? Do Emily and I need to dress alike?"

"I don't think so," Mom answered. "It's not that kind of wedding."

"What about colors?" I asked. "Do you know what colors you want?"

Mom shook her head. "I haven't thought about it yet."

I went into the hallway and pulled my laptop out of my bag. "We need to get on this right away, or I will never hear the end of it from Alexis."

I opened up a wedding website on my screen and searched "June wedding ideas."

"You can do that?" Mom asked.

I nodded. "How did you not know about this?" I asked her.

We spent the next hour scrolling through web pages and giggling, and then we started playing popular wedding songs and dancing around the kitchen. It would have been the perfect night if there hadn't been a nagging thought in the back of my head: *I'd better enjoy this time with Mom while it lasts!*

CHAPTER 4

Dancing with Donny

They're doing what?" Mia asked me the next morning on the bus.

"They're getting married as soon as school ends," I repeated.

Mia shook her head. "Does Alexis know?"

"I made Mom e-mail her last night," I replied. "I didn't want to be the one to do it. She is going to freak out bad enough as it is! I'm hoping the worst will be out of her system by lunchtime."

"Don't count on it," Mia said.

I heard George's voice behind me, and I turned around and looked over my seat.

"Hey, I can play basketball on Sunday," I said.

"Cool. Three o'clock?" he asked.

"Sure," I said, and then I turned back to Mia.

She was holding up her phone. There was a group text from Alexis: URGENT! Brown-Green wedding has moved up to 6/26. We need to set a date to test flavors ASAP. Pls respond. More talk at lunch!

I laughed. "Oh boy," I said. "We are in for it!"

Alexis wasn't kidding around. She didn't mention the wedding at all during gym class, but at lunchtime she slid a checklist over to me as soon as I sat down.

"I e-mailed the same checklist to your mom last night," Alexis said. "I need you to push her for me, Katie. I need answers to these questions right away! I listed them in order of importance."

I glanced at the list. *Venue for the wedding service? Venue for the reception? Number of guests? Wedding colors?* The list went on and on.

"I'm glad I'm not planning this," I said. "I'll talk to her tonight. Oh, I can check one thing off the list for you. I'm her maid of honor!"

Mia and Emma had joined us by that point.

"Katie, that's so exciting!" Emma squealed.

"I will help you pick out a dress," Mia promised.

"Thanks," I said. "I think usually the bride picks out the dresses, but I bet Mom would be relieved to have your help. I honestly have no idea what to wear. But thankfully, Mom says I don't have to throw her a bachelorette party or anything like that."

"What about a bridal shower?" Emma asked. "Those are really fun."

I felt my stomach do a little flip. "A bridal shower? I have no idea how to do that."

"There is literally no time for a bridal shower," Alexis said. "I think your mom knows that. But as maid of honor, it's your responsibility to make sure everything else goes smoothly."

"*Everything* else?" I asked.

"Yes," Alexis said. She tapped the list in front of me. "Talk to your mother!"

"I will! I promise!" I said.

❧

That night, I prepared the meal from the boxed kit that Mom had been getting lately while I waited for her to come home from work. She trusted me now to cook on my own, and the meal kits were just enough food for two people and easy to make. When she got home, I had the table set with finished plates of chicken with vegetable couscous.

"Katie, this looks delicious," Mom said, after she'd washed up and sat down. "Thank you!"

"No problem," I said. "I wanted to get dinner out of the way so you and I could talk about the wedding. If I don't, I'm afraid what Alexis will do."

Mom laughed. "Yes, I got her e-mails. Do you want to talk now?"

I took out the Alexis checklist. "Shoot."

"Well, Jeff and I want to have the ceremony in the park, where he proposed," she said. "Jeff's getting the permit now, but it shouldn't be a problem."

"That sounds nice," I said, and wrote "park" into the chart.

"The Women's Club is right across the street, and they have a lovely banquet hall with a kitchen and a dance floor," Mom continued. "We thought about having the reception in the park too, but doing it at the Women's Club would be so much easier. And the bathrooms are a lot nicer than the park ones. And we checked and they are not booked yet on the twenty-sixth."

I wrote "Women's Club" on the chart. "All right, what about colors?" I asked her.

"I was thinking . . . pink," Mom said.

I raised my eyebrows. "Really? But green is your favorite color."

"I know, but . . . I've used green before," she said, and I knew she meant at her first wedding. "Besides, you'll look so pretty in a pink dress. And pink is such a sweet and romantic color."

"Pink it is," I said, thinking that the Cupcake Club would be happy to hear that.

"And that's about all I've got figured out," Mom said, spearing a piece of chicken with her fork.

"That should be enough to satisfy Alexis for a little while," I said. "Now that we know the colors, we can narrow down the cupcake flavor."

"Oh, that reminds me," Mom said. "I scheduled a wedding thing for this Sunday, and I need you there. It's at three o'clock."

"What is it?" I asked, thinking of my basketball plans with George.

"It's a surprise," Mom said, and her eyes were twinkling. "I think you'll like it."

"Well, I'm supposed to hang out with George, but if it's a wedding thing . . ."

"Thanks, Katie! This means a lot to me!" Mom said.

❖

We finished our dinner, and I texted George: Can't do basketball Sunday. Wedding thing with Mom.

He texted back: K.

Uh-oh, I thought. The dreaded "K." The response you gave when you weren't happy with what the person texting you told you. It was colder than a sad face because at least a sad face showed some emotion. The "K" was just so cold and robotic.

We'll do it soon! I texted him, and waited for a response. I didn't get one.

Oh well. George was the least of my problems right now. I had a wedding to get ready for!

✿

I was surprised on Sunday when Mom and I drove up to Jeff's house and Emily ran out.

"What's this all about?" I asked, before Emily got into the car.

"You'll see," Mom replied, and then Emily slid into the back seat.

"I'm so excited," Emily said. "Do you know where we're going, Katie? Dad wouldn't tell me."

"No idea," I admitted.

"I think we're going to get dresses," Emily guessed. "Are we going to get dresses, Sharon?"

I winced. One thing that was hard to get used to was Emily calling my mom by her first name.

"I'm not giving away the surprise," Mom said. "Not yet."

This is going to be an awesome surprise, I thought, *especially if Mom is going to all this trouble to keep it a secret.*

She drove down the street and then got onto Harrison Road. I suddenly had a thought.

"We're going to Stonebrook!" I said. I know because that's where Dessert Dad's restaurant is, and a bunch of fancy shops, and Mom takes Harrison Road when she drives me there. "I bet we *are* going to look at dresses."

Mom didn't say anything—she just smiled—and I tried to think of what else was in Stonebrook. A shoe store. A greeting card shop. An ice-cream parlor. None of those seemed really exciting.

I kept my eyes peeled out the window as we drove down the main street, past Chez Daniel, and turned a corner. Mom pulled into a parking lot of a tall white house that had been turned into a business.

Emily saw the sign before I did.

"The Moonlight Dance Studio!" she squealed. "Are we really getting dancing lessons?"

"You and Katie are, just in time for the wedding," Mom said happily.

I heard the sound of tires screeching in my head. I am a terrible dancer. "Dancing lessons? Why do we need dancing lessons?"

"There will be a deejay at the wedding and dancing," Mom replied. "And Emily was telling Jeff about how some of her friends took a dance class here to help them get through school dances and

40

things like that. So we thought it would be fun for you girls to try it."

"Oh, thank you!" Emily cried. "Ivy and Samantha both took dance classes here, and they said it was so much fun! And now Katie and I will be great dancers at the wedding."

I will never be a great dancer, I thought, but I held in my protests because Mom and Emily looked so happy.

"So this is a one-time thing?" I asked.

Mom nodded. "This class is for social dancing, but if you wanted to learn something fancier, we could bring you back."

"Let's see how this goes," I said, and I started to get out of the car. Mom stayed put. "You're not coming in?"

"Jeff and I are going for a run," she said. "I'll pick you up in ninety minutes."

Ninety minutes! I thought, and I stifled a groan. Emily and I walked up to the front door (well, I walked and Emily practically skipped with joy), entered, and approached the front desk.

"Um, Katie Brown and Emily Green," I said to the young woman with the messy top bun behind the counter.

She quickly tapped a few keys on her computer.

"Ah, yes, here you are. You're in Dancing with Donny. That's the second door on the right."

"I can't believe this," Emily whispered as we made our way to the door. "Donny is supposed to be awesome! This is going to be amazing!"

We stepped into a dance studio with a polished wooden floor. About six other people were milling around: a couple of teenagers, some kids Emily's age, and two gray-haired ladies. Nobody was saying anything, and there was an awkward vibe in the air.

Suddenly, pop music started blaring, and a guy stepped through a door on the opposite side of the room. He danced toward us in sparkly silver sneakers, his wavy blond hair sliding in front of his eyes. His T-shirt read DANCE WITH DONNY.

Donny did a spin, and then he dropped into a split and held his arms out wide and smiled. Emily and the other people started clapping. Then he jumped up, took a bow, and used a little remote control to stop the music.

"Hey, everybody. I'm Donny Davis!" he said, and then he paused, so I started clapping. He smiled again. "Welcome to Dancing with Donny! Before we begin, I'd like to see where we're all at, so when the music starts, dance!" I suddenly felt a little nervous.

He turned the music back on. The older ladies held hands and started spinning each other around. Emily did this jumping sort of thing, and I did my usual move, which is to bounce up and down on my knees without moving my feet, while snapping my fingers. After a minute, the music stopped.

"Okay then, we'll be starting with the basics," Donny said. "By the end of the class, you'll learn some basic moves that will make you look smooth on the dance floor. And we all want to look smooth on the dance floor, right?"

Everyone nodded.

"Great! Now let me see you line up and stand facing me, with your feet shoulder-width apart," Donny instructed.

We obeyed.

"I'm going to start the music again. First, close your eyes. Feel the beat," he instructed.

The music started again. I listened for the beat. *Thump, thump, thump.*

"Now open your eyes. For our first step, I want you to move your right foot to the side. Bring your left foot to meet it. Tap your left foot, and then move your left foot to the side."

He did it slowly, and we all copied him.

"Step, tap, step," Donny said. "Step, tap, step."

I glanced at Emily, and she smiled at me. So far, this was easy!

"Now we're going to mix it up a little bit," Donny continued. "The next time you step, step back with your right foot. Then bring your left foot back to meet it. Tap. Then bring your left foot forward, making a diagonal line."

That was a little harder for me to manage, but after a few tries, I figured it out.

Step, tap, step, I repeated in my head.

"Look at you superstars go!" Donny cheered. "All right, now we're going to add some upper body movements."

Donny showed us how we could swing our shoulders when we moved our feet, and bend our elbows and swing our arms across our bodies. I glanced around the room, and I had to admit that everyone looked way cooler than they had when Donny had us dance on our own in the beginning. Maybe he was onto something.

"Feel free to add some hand movements, as long as they go with the music," Donny instructed, straightening his hands and making some karate-like jabs in the air. Next to me, Emily started winding her arms together like snakes, and we laughed.

"There you go! Now we're having fun!" Donny

cheered. "Okay, you're on your own. Let me see you take this song through to the end."

Step, tap, step. Step, tap, step. One of the teenage boys twirled around on one foot on the last step, and I was feeling pretty confident, so I tried it.

"Nice, Katie!" Emily called out over the music, and I smiled at her.

When the song ended, the boy who had twirled around raised his hand. "I thought we were going to learn some popular dances in this class. Like flossing."

Flossing was this dance that went viral online, where your feet don't move but your hips are moving, and it looks like your body is magically passing through your outstretched arms. I have never been able to do it.

"I know an even better dance," Donny said. "You've heard of the Dougie? I call this one the Donny. I usually save it for my advanced classes, but I think you guys are ready."

I looked at Emily and raised my eyebrows. Were we ready?

Donny played a hip-hop song and began by simply rocking his hips. Then he started pointing up at the sky, spinning, and hopping backward and forward.

"What do you think?" he asked. "My students say it's their favorite."

Everybody kind of muttered their answers, and Donny launched into teaching us in slow motion. It was kind of complicated, but Emily got it down perfectly. I went back to step, tap, step, and the teenage boy just started flossing on his own.

Then the gray-haired ladies asked about a dance called the Hustle from the 1970s, and Donny didn't know it, but one of them remembered it, and she ended up trying to teach us. That one was so complicated! You had to roll your arms around each other, fast, in a move called the egg beater, and even flap your arms like a chicken. I got the arm moves down just fine, but I couldn't do any of the foot movements at the same time. I think that's my dancing problem.

"Great job, everyone!" Donny said when class was over. "I hope you'll be at my next social dancing class, *More* Dancing with Donny!"

Emily and I got a drink from the water cooler and then waited outside for Mom and Jeff to pick us up.

"That was pretty fun," Emily said. "Thanks for doing this with me, Katie."

"You're welcome," I said, and for the first time,

I felt like I might know what it was like to be a big sister. And that was pretty nice.

Emily took a deep breath. She glanced at me quickly and then looked down at her shoes.

"Were you going to say something else?" I asked.

Emily nodded. Then she looked at me again. "I've been getting really nervous about all the changes coming up," she said. "And . . . a little jealous of you too."

I was shocked. "Jealous of me?" I asked. "Why?"

Emily gave a little laugh. "I know it sounds silly, but I was jealous that now you are going to have my dad around all the time. And you're so smart, and interesting and cool—"

"Cool? Me?" I blurted it out before I could even stop myself. Emily laughed and nodded.

"Yes! You've got the most awesome friends, and the Cupcake Club!"

"The Cupcake Club is pretty cool," I admitted. "And I've been a little jealous of you, too. I was envious that you get your mom to yourself all the time, and now I have to share mine."

"Wow, I never thought about that," Emily said. We were both quiet for a moment, lost in our own thoughts.

"At any rate, I feel a little better knowing you

were worrying about the same things," I finally said. "It's easier to go through these things if you're not alone."

"Definitely," Emily said. And she smiled up at me. I felt more like a big sister than ever.

CHAPTER 5

More Changes!

So, how was it?" Mom asked as Emily and I slid into the back seat of the car. Jeff was in the front seat with her, and I noticed that neither of them were dressed in running clothes, which seemed odd.

"It was fun," I said. "But I don't think I'll be dancing the Donny at your wedding, if that's okay."

"You can dance however you want, as long as you're having fun," Jeff said. He reached over and squeezed Mom's hand, and they smiled at each other.

"What's for dinner?" I asked Mom. "I'm starving."

"We placed a takeout order at Golden Palace," Mom replied. "And we're bringing it back to our house. I hope that's okay."

"That is awesome," I said. "Did you get spring rolls?"

"Yes," Mom replied.

"And wonton soup?" I asked.

Jeff answered this time. "Yes. And chicken with broccoli and fried rice and scallion pancakes and steamed dumplings."

"WE SHALL FEAST!" I exclaimed too loudly. I guess I had worked up some energy during that dance lesson. Emily giggled, and Mom and Jeff smiled at each other again.

We swung by the restaurant on the way home, and Jeff ran in to get the order and came out carrying two very large bags of food. When we got home I set the table without being asked because I was so happy to be back at home, eating food that I loved. And I was happy that all the surprises for the day were over.

Or so I thought.

The whole time we slurped our soup, Mom and Jeff were staring at each other like they had a big secret to share.

"What is up with you two?" I asked.

Jeff grabbed Mom's hand, and they each took a deep breath.

"We didn't go running this afternoon," Mom

said. She looked at Jeff, and they said the next thing together.

"We bought a house!"

I couldn't believe what I was hearing. *A house?*

"You mean, for us?" I asked. "I thought we were going to stay in this house, Mom. You promised! Why didn't you tell me about this before?"

"Oh, Katie, I'm sorry," Mom said. "It's just that—"

I didn't wait for her to answer. I ran out of the kitchen, into my bedroom, and slammed the door behind me. Then I started crying again, just like I had the other day.

They bought a house! That meant we were moving, just like Alexis had guessed. Leaving this house forever. The house I'd lived in since I was a baby. Wasn't getting a whole new family a big enough change? Why did we have to move, too?

I cried some more, part of me wondering why Mom wasn't coming upstairs to talk to me. My stomach rumbled, but I didn't want to go downstairs. I stayed on my bed, tears streaming down my face, until the sun stopped streaming through my window.

Then I heard the front door close, and I peeked through the window to see Mom talking with Jeff and Emily in front of Jeff's car. Finally. I walked downstairs. Mom had left the cartons of food on the kitchen counter, like I'd guessed she would, and I piled a plate high with chicken, broccoli, and rice. It was cold, but I didn't care. I shoveled it down.

When Mom walked back in, I was opening up a fortune cookie.

"Oh look. It says 'You will move out of your childhood home and live a miserable life,'" I told her.

Mom sat down next to me. "Katie, I'm sorry. I should have told you about this first, just the two of us. I forgot what a big change this might mean for you."

Those were good words to hear. I nodded. "You're right. You should have talked to me first."

"I know," Mom said. "I thought it would be a special surprise. But I realize now that I've been so caught up in the wedding planning that I haven't been checking in with you to see how you're doing."

"You haven't!" I blurted out. "I have so many questions!"

Then I let it all spill—my worries about breakfast for dinner, and pajama night, and not having alone time with Mom. We talked for a long time about all that stuff, and Mom pinkie swore with me that we would still have special times together, just me and her.

Then my eyes filled with tears again. "But what about—what about the house?" I asked. "Is it in Maple Grove? Will I have to change schools?"

"Oh, Katie, I think you'll really love it!" Mom said. "It's right here in Maple Grove, right off the running trail in Willow Brook Park."

Okay, now Mom had my interest. That is one of my favorite trails. It's a beautiful neighborhood there, with so many trees. And the houses are such pretty colors!

"Really?" I asked.

She nodded. "Jeff and I hadn't planned on buying a house together yet, I swear," she said. "But we were running a couple of weeks ago and saw the 'For Sale' sign being put up in front of it. We toured it, and it's perfect! So we just made an offer, and it got accepted right away."

She took out her phone and held up the screen to show me a two-story house with a wraparound front porch and pale-yellow shingles.

"Isn't it pretty?" she asked. "It's a little bigger than this place. Emily will have her own room when she comes to visit, but you'll get the bigger room for your bedroom, of course. And it will be a fresh start for the four of us, as a family."

I understood everything Mom was saying, and I wanted to be happy about the new house—I really did! But I mostly felt sad and confused and worried.

"When are we moving?" I asked.

Mom bit her lip. "That's the thing. It looks like we need to move at the end of June, right after the wedding."

My eyes got wide. "Are you serious?" I asked. "And you thought the most important thing to do today was send me and Emily to a dance lesson?"

Mom laughed. "I know, it all seems kind of silly. But it feels *right* to me, Katie. I can't explain it. I've been working so hard at the practice all these years, and I'm going to take some time off starting in June. And Jeff's got lots of friends who can help us move. It's going to be fine."

She stood up and opened her arms. "Can I have a hug?"

I got up and fell into her arms. I gripped her probably too tightly.

Please let things always be like this, I thought, even though I knew that wasn't possible.

I went up to my room and lay down on my bed, staring at the ceiling. There was the crack that looked like a lightning bolt, and there was the old water stain that reminded me of a winking moon. My eyes stung as I realized that soon they'd be gone from my life forever. This whole house would belong to someone else. Would the kid sleeping in this room next even notice the winking moon? Or would the new owners paint over it before that kid even got a chance to see it?

As I gazed around at my bookcase, my dresser with clothes spilling out, and the closet so stuffed with all my old toys that I couldn't close it, the thought hit me that I was going to somehow have to pack all of it up and move it to the new house. I groaned and covered my face with my pillow.

How was I going to get through this?

CHAPTER 6

Cooking Is Soothing

I really need to have a talk with your mom," Alexis said the next day at lunch. "What she's trying to do is impossible! But at least we have a baking session planned for Wednesday."

"I know," I said. "But she's so happy! She's smiling all the time. She doesn't seem stressed out at all."

"What about you, Katie? Are you happy?" Emma asked with her blue eyes full of concern.

"I—I'm confused," I said. "I'm kind of freaking out that things with Mom are going to change. And it's going to be so weird to be living in the same house as Jeff! And even though the new house looks really nice, I'm going to miss my old one. It's just a lot of things changing all at once, you know?"

"Well, you've got us to help you through it," Mia said. "That's one thing that won't change."

"Thanks, Mia," I said. "If I weren't eating a sandwich, I would hug you right now."

"Where is the house again?" Alexis asked.

"On Willow Brook Road, right off the park," I answered. I took my school laptop out of my bag. "Let me see if I can get it on here," I said. The laptops were set so that you couldn't use them to go on social media sites, but you could do research on them, and I wanted a bigger picture than the one on my phone. Luckily, I was able to connect to the real estate listing. I called it up and my friends gathered around me.

"That is so cute," Mia said. "I love that porch!"

I scrolled to the kitchen. "And look. The kitchen has an island! We'll have more room for baking."

"Which one will your room be?" Mia asked me.

I scrolled through the photos until I found it. Right now it didn't look like much—four white walls and a wood floor, with a window overlooking the park. But it was bright and airy-looking, I thought, with more room than I had already.

"Ooh, Katie, we can paint your room with you before you move in!" Emma cried. "We can help you pick out colors and decorate."

I kind of liked that idea. My bedroom still had the flowered wallpaper that my mom had put up when I was a baby. It might be fun to design my own room. But first . . .

"I can't even think about decorating my new room," I said. "I've got to pack up my old room first. *And* help get the wedding together."

Alexis ripped a sheet of paper from her notebook and drew four columns.

"Okay, let's figure this out," she began. "You need to pack up your stuff."

She wrote "pack up" in the first column. Then she wrote her name under it. "I would love to help you organize your room for the move," she said.

"Really?" I asked. "It sounds like a nightmare to me."

Alexis grinned. "Sometimes I fall asleep at night by imagining I am packing things into boxes and putting them away," she confessed. "Weird, I know, but I am totally psyched to do it."

She looked back down at the paper. "What kind of wedding stuff do you have to do? The Cupcake Club is making the cupcakes," she said.

"Well, I have to find a maid of honor dress," I replied. "And I know, Mia, you said you would help me. But I can't imagine having to go shopping at a bunch of different stores to find the perfect one."

Mia's face brightened. "Then don't!" she said. "Why don't I design and sew a dress for you?"

My mouth dropped open. "Would you really do that for me?"

She nodded. "It'll be fun! I'll just need to measure you, and then I'll draw it up, make a pattern, and sew it. You said the wedding color's pink, right? You'll look pretty in pink."

"Wow," I said. "That's amazing, Mia!"

Alexis wrote Mia's name under "maid of honor dress."

"Put me under 'decorate new room,'" Emma said, practically bouncing in her seat. "I mean, we can all help, but I'd love to be in charge of it."

"You guys are awesome," I said. "The best friends I could ever ask for."

"I know you are, but what am I," Alexis said, which was so silly and so unlike her that we all busted out laughing.

"I'll bring my measuring tape to our baking session on Wednesday," Mia said.

"And I will start a new idea board of cute room ideas and share it with everybody," Emma said.

"Are we set for the baking session?" Alexis asked. "I don't think we decided on flavors."

"Well, since Mom decided on pink, the apple idea is out," I said. "So I was thinking that vanilla with strawberry filling might be nice. And we could also test the Earl Grey cupcakes."

"How about we bake at my house?" Mia asked.

I shook my head. "I think we should do it at my place. I have everything we need for the test. And besides . . ." I paused. "I think we need to bake at least one last time in the house."

Everybody got quiet, and I knew they were thinking of all the happy memories we'd had in my kitchen. I knew I was.

"That kitchen is where your mom made the cupcake you brought to school that first day," Emma said.

I nodded. "The P-B-and-J cupcake. The one that brought us all together."

We all got quiet again.

"Then it is very cool that we are testing your mom's wedding cupcakes in that kitchen," Alexis said. "It's like the beginning and ending to a story."

"Not an ending, really," Mia said quickly. "It'll be a whole new story after Katie moves. An even better one, maybe."

"I hope so," I said. "I definitely want to live happily ever after!"

❀

Mia got off the bus with me on Wednesday afternoon. Emma and Alexis had to take the bus to Emma's house, where Emma's oldest brother, Sam, was going to give them a ride.

Mia whipped out a measuring tape from her backpack as soon as we got inside my house.

"Okay, quickly, let me measure you," she said, and she wrapped the measuring tape around my waist.

"Hey, that tickles!" I cried, giggling.

"Stand still!" Mia commanded, and I did my best as she measured me all the way around and up and down. She made notes on her phone.

"Last night I researched some dresses, and I made some sketches," she said. "I know you're busy, but maybe tomorrow after school you can come to my house, and we can go over the design?"

"Sure, that works," I said. "Or you can come over Friday. Mom and I have planned our first 'pizza-and-packing' weekend. I'm hoping there will be more pizza than packing."

Mia frowned. "I'll be at my dad's," she said. "But I'll definitely help you the next weekend I'm home. Don't worry, Katie."

"It's okay," I said. "I'm so thrilled that you're

helping me with this dress. It's going to be perfect!"

The doorbell rang, and I opened it for Alexis and Emma.

"Hi," Emma said, but Alexis didn't say anything. She marched right up to my room. I raised my eyebrows at Mia and Emma.

"Alexis, what are you doing?" I called up the stairs.

"Oh my *word*, Katie!" Alexis called back. She appeared at the top of the stairs. "You have so much stuff in your room!"

"Well, I've lived here all my life," I said.

"I've never seen so many stuffed animals!" she shot back.

"Well, I'm an only child," I argued. "My grandparents like to spoil me."

"And you are obsessed with stuffed animals," Mia added.

"Well, they're so cute," I said.

Alexis came down the stairs. "That's fine," she said. "Now I know how many boxes to bring with me. Can I come on Saturday morning?"

I sighed. "Sure. Mom and I planned to pack anyway," I said.

She nodded. "Sure, we'll pack. But first we've got to purge."

"Purge? You mean like get rid of stuff?" I felt panic rising. "What kind of stuff?"

"All kinds of stuff," Alexis replied. "I'd say you could get rid of about ninety percent of—"

Emma took my arm and pulled me toward the kitchen. "We're here to bake, aren't we?" she asked. "Let's make some cupcakes."

I was grateful to Emma for changing the subject. Once in the kitchen, I started pulling out bowls and cupcake tins. The mixer was already plugged in and ready to go.

"So the simplest thing to do for the strawberry-and-vanilla cupcakes would be to bake vanilla cupcakes and then use the cupcake plunger to poke a hole in them and add strawberry jam," I said. "But the other day at Chez Daniel, I made strawberry mousse, and I thought that might be fancier to go inside."

"Mousse is like fancy whipped cream?" Alexis asked.

"Kind of," I said.

"We'd have to refrigerate the cupcakes, then," she pointed out.

"I know," I said. "But it might be worth it to make them extra fancy. Since it's a wedding and all."

"Can we test them with both the jam and the

mousse?" Alexis asked. "I can work on the vanilla cake batter."

"And I'd like to work on the Earl Grey," Emma piped up. "I think it will be a really cool flavor."

"I'll get started on frosting when the mixer's free," Mia said. "In the meantime, I'm putting together an idea board of pink wedding cupcake toppers that we can look at."

Mia sat down at the table and opened up her laptop. Alexis preheated the oven and started filling cupcake tins with liners. I took a container of chopped-up strawberries I'd prepared the night before and took it to the stovetop. Emma joined me with a small saucepan of milk.

"So, I warm the milk first and then add the teabags?" Emma asked.

"Right," I said. "And you let the teabags steep for about five minutes and then squeeze them really good to get all the tea out. Then you'll use that milk when you make your batter."

"Got it," Emma said. She called over to Alexis, "You can use the mixer first, Lex, and then I'll use it for the Earl Grey batter."

"Sounds good," Alexis said, and she began creaming butter, sugar, and eggs together for the vanilla cake.

We didn't do a lot of cupcake testing anymore because we had already perfected so many awesome flavors. It cost money to do the tests because we had to buy new ingredients. But it was worth it if we came up with a new flavor that people liked. Sometimes word would get around about an unusual flavor, like our piña colada cupcakes we made last summer. They became a big hit at barbecues.

I was glad that we were trying out two new ideas for the wedding. That would help make it really special.

The kitchen got quiet as we worked. We'd made so many cupcakes since we started the club that we could practically do it in our sleep. Alexis got her batter for the vanilla cupcakes into the oven, and then Emma started mixing the Earl Grey batter. I had turned the strawberries into a purée and had it cooling in the fridge. Then I set up a bowl with my old-school hand mixer to make the mousse, so Mia could use the stand mixer for the frosting.

"You're all set," I told her.

Mia nodded toward her laptop on the table. "You guys, take a look at the cupcake images there while I make the frosting. What if we put strawberry-buttercream frosting on the vanilla cupcakes and topped them with white vanilla-buttercream roses?

Then we could put vanilla-buttercream frosting on the Earl Grey, and top those with pink strawberry-buttercream roses."

"Ooh, I like that," Emma said. "We can do alternating layers of pink and white on the cupcake tower."

"I'm still finding a tower big enough to hold more than a hundred cupcakes," Alexis said. "We might need a smaller tower, with plates of cupcakes around it."

"That would still be pretty," Emma said.

Mia finished her frosting, I finished the mousse, and we cleaned up our mess while the frosting and mousse chilled and the two trays of cupcakes baked and cooled. Before we were ready to start decorating, Mom walked in carrying two pizza boxes and a white takeout bag. We helped her get the stuff to the kitchen table.

"I figured you guys might want a dinner break," Mom said. "It's pizza. I think it's going to be pizza a lot for the next few days. But I did get a salad." She lifted up the paper bag.

"I will never get sick of pizza!" I promised, and I grabbed some plates out of the cabinet. Mia got the forks, and Alexis and Emma got the glasses. My friends knew their way around our kitchen.

We all sat down and dug in, and Mia showed Mom a picture of a pink-and-white cupcake tower that inspired her plan.

"At first we thought it should be a surprise," Mia said. "But then we agreed the bride should know what her cupcake cake was going to look like! What do you think?"

"It's lovely," Mom said. "I'm sure whatever you girls do is going to be beautiful. My head is starting to spin! Mia, your mom offered to take me dress shopping this weekend, but I've got to start packing, or Katie and I will never get out of here."

"I'm coming to help Katie on Saturday," Alexis said. "I'm sure you could spare a few hours. Getting a dress is important."

"I suppose you're right," Mom said. "Thanks, Alexis."

"Mom, Mia is going to design and make my dress for me," I told her. "Isn't that awesome?"

"Mia, that is amazing," Mom said. "You have to let me pay you."

"I'd like to do it as a wedding present," Mia said.

Mom's eyes filled with tears. "I am so lucky that Katie has such wonderful friends," she said. "But, Mia, I insist on paying for the materials. That's only fair."

Then Alexis tried to pin Mom down on more wedding details, and we finished our pizza. We cleared the table and got to work decorating. First, I divided the vanilla-buttercream frosting in half and mixed in some strawberry purée in one half until it turned pale pink. Then I used an injector—kind of like a big syringe—to get the strawberry mousse inside the vanilla cupcakes.

In the meantime, Mia and Emma frosted the Earl Grey cupcakes. Mia took some of the strawberry frosting and piped tiny roses on one of them. Then Alexis piped strawberry frosting onto the vanilla cupcakes, and Mia decorated them with perfect white roses.

We called in Mom when we were finished. "They're beautiful!" she exclaimed.

Alexis cut the cupcakes in half so we could all try some. We tried the Earl Grey first.

"What is this flavor?" Mom asked. "Is it some kind of flower?"

"Earl Grey tea," I told her.

"It's very nice," Mom said. "I wouldn't have guessed tea."

"The flavor could be stronger," Emma agreed.

Then we all tried the strawberry-mousse cupcakes.

"Oh my goodness," Mom said. "These are divine!"

"Yeah, that mousse is a million-dollar business idea waiting to happen," Alexis said.

"Maybe we should just do all the cupcakes with the mousse," I said. "We can still do two different frosting colors, though."

"That could work," Mom said. "Oh, and can you make a gluten-free dozen too? Jeff's brother's family doesn't do wheat."

Alexis shook her head. "Well, we definitely can, but you forgot to mention that in our menu discussion, Mrs. B," she said. "Is there anything else I need to know about the guests' dietary restrictions? Any vegans? Paleos? Ketos?"

Mom looked bewildered. "Um . . . no? But I'll check."

I picked up a cupcake, stood, and held it out.

"I'd like to make a toast," I said. "To this kitchen! We've made many good cupcakes here."

Mom and my friends grabbed cupcakes and stood up.

"Hear! Hear!" Mom said.

"And it won't matter when you move, because we'll make even better cupcakes there, there!" Alexis joked.

We all laughed, and I didn't cry, even though I thought I might.

A kitchen was just a room. But my friends—they were forever. And at that moment, I had a feeling that everything was going to be all right.

CHAPTER 7

What's Up with George?

That's weird," I said the next day as I sat next to Mia on the bus.

"What's weird?" Mia asked.

"Wes and Aziz are sitting behind us," I said.

"So?" Mia asked.

"So, George and Ken *always* sit right behind us," I told her. "They have been doing it forever."

I craned my head to look at the back of the bus. "And now George is sitting over there with Eddie and Sofia. What's he doing there?"

"Probably Ken is out sick," Mia guessed. "So he took another seat."

"Ken has been sick before," I pointed out. "George never gives up his seat because somebody else will take it. Like Wes and Aziz just did."

Wes stuck his head over the seat. "Are you talking about us? I heard our names."

"No," I lied. "And, anyway, stop eavesdropping!"

"If you are accusing me of eavesdropping, then you must have been talking about us," Wes countered. "Otherwise, how did you know that I knew that you said my name?"

Now Mia turned around. "Wes, it is way too early for this," she said, and Wes ducked his head behind the seat without another word. Mia has a way of quieting people with just a look. It is awesome to have a cool friend.

I lowered my voice. "It's just . . . things have been weird with George lately," I said. "It's like he doesn't want to be friends anymore."

"Has he been mean to you?" Mia asked. "Because I will let him know that nobody—"

"No, nothing like that," I said. "He's just acting weird. I can't explain it. And it didn't help that I had to cancel our basketball game last weekend. He's barely spoken to me since then."

"Aha," Mia said. "Was that the first time you canceled plans with him?"

"No," I admitted. "Ever since Mom and Jeff announced their engagement, I've been so busy with stuff."

72

"Then maybe George is feeling left out," Mia said.

I hadn't considered this. "It's possible," I said. "Come to think of it, I guess I haven't been talking to *him* much anymore, either. I'm usually talking to you guys about wedding and moving stuff."

A scene popped into my head from just the other day in the hallway. Alexis had been at my locker, showing me an app with packing tips she'd found, and George had run up. He'd looked like he wanted to say something, but when I'd looked up from Alexis's phone, he had already gone.

"So maybe George is just feeling ignored," Mia said. "I would too, if you were canceling plans on me and stuff like that."

I nodded. "Okay, but what do I do? It's not like I'm going to suddenly have free time before the wedding."

Suddenly a huge grin spread across Mia's face. "I've got it!" she said. "Why don't you ask him to help the Cupcake Club with the dessert table? That way he'll be part of the wedding, and with George helping, me and Emma and Alexis might be able to dance and have fun a little bit."

I frowned. "So you want me to ask George to work for free?"

"No! I mean, he can still have fun too. But this way, he'll be part of it," she said.

I nodded again. "That might work," I said. "I'll ask him."

I figured I'd ask him that day, but I didn't have a chance. There was a food fight in the cafeteria at lunchtime (a sign that the school year was coming to an end; everyone was restless). It was mostly seventh graders who threw the food. I got away with only some ketchup on the sleeve of my hoodie, but it was chaos.

After school, George sat in the back of the bus again, and I sat in the front with Mia. I took the bus all the way to her house. Except for the dogs, it was quiet when we got there. Mia's mom was working in her office, her stepdad was still at work, and her brother and cousin were out.

"Let's go to my room," Mia said, and I followed her upstairs.

Mia's bedroom looked like something from a magazine. It hadn't always looked that way, but her stepdad, Eddie, helped her do it. The walls were turquoise, and they'd painted all the old furniture that came with the house a glossy black.

"I guess it's going to be fun to decorate my room from scratch," I said.

"Is your new room going to look like a rainbow exploded in it, too?" Mia teased.

I picked up a pillow from her bed and tossed it at her. "I can't help it if I love *all* the colors. Why do I have to pick one?"

"Well, at least we only have to worry about one color for your dress—pink," Mia said. "I have a few ideas for you."

I clapped my hands together. "I have never been so excited about a dress before in my life," I said. "I can't wait to see this one!"

We sat down on the bed, and Mia took out her sketchbook. She turned to a page of a girl with brown hair (and no face) wearing a long, straight dress down to the floor and straps that went around the neck.

"This one is simple and classy," she said.

I nodded. "I get it. It's nice."

Then she showed me a sketch of a sleeveless dress with a short, flouncy skirt and lace around the collar.

"This one's more fun and flirty," she said.

"It is," I agreed. "But do I need to look more serious to be a maid of honor?"

Mia turned the page. "No, you can look as serious or silly as you want—within reason, of course! Okay, now here's the third one. . . ."

I gasped. The dress had fluttery cap sleeves, and a flouncy skirt with what looked like layers of fabric underneath it. The color was a soft pink, with darker pink roses scattered across the skirt.

"I love it!" I squealed. "I have never wanted to be a princess before, but I would *so* be a princess in that dress."

Mia smiled. "I had a feeling you would like that one the best. It's not too fancy, and it even kind of matches the cupcakes."

"Wait a second," I said. "Do princesses have to wear heels? Do maids of honor have to wear them?"

"I think this dress would look perfect with pink flats," she said. "Or something called a kitten heel. It's a little tiny heel that will make the outfit dressier, but you'll still be really comfortable. We can find some online and send the links to your mom."

I hugged her. "Mia, this is beautiful. Perfect. Are you sure you can make it in just a few weeks?"

She nodded. "Yes. I'm excited about it. It's going to look great in my portfolio. You're going to have to let me take lots of pictures!"

"You can take all the pictures you want," I promised her. I looked down at the sketch again, and then I looked at Mia.

"Wow, this is really happening," I said.

Mia nodded. "Yes."

"I'm still kind of worried about it," I admitted.

"I know," Mia said. "But I remember you once told me how lucky I was to have two dads, and you were right. I was pretty miserable when my parents got divorced and my mom moved out here. And I got a stepdad and a stepbrother pretty quick. But Eddie is so cool. He does a lot for me. And now, you'll have Jeff. And maybe that's not so bad."

"And I have Marc Daniel Brown, too," I reminded her. "So I guess now we'll both have two dads."

Mia held out her hand. "The Two Dads Club," she said.

I shook her hand. "The Two Dads Club," I repeated. "Um, shouldn't we have a cooler handshake than this? Like, a secret handshake?"

"I don't think I know how to do one," she said, but we tried wiggling our fingers and moving our hands up and down, and it was so ridiculous that we slid onto the floor laughing.

"You're going to have to be president of the Two Dads Club," I told her. "Because I am still new at it."

"Okay," Mia said. "You can be vice president."

I know we were just kidding about the Two Dads Club, but it made me feel good to know that Mia had experienced something close to what I was going through. I wanted to believe that things would turn out okay. But even if they didn't, at least I had Mia to help me.

CHAPTER 8

A Private Tour

Even though it was our first pizza-and-packing weekend, I had to report for pastry duty at Chez Daniel on Saturday morning. I helped Melissa make cream puffs and blackberry tarts. While we worked, we talked about Mom's upcoming wedding and the move and everything.

"You know, Katie, you should probably take some time off from the restaurant," she said as we wrapped up. "You are a terrific help to me, but it sounds like you have a lot on your plate."

I would miss working at Chez Daniel, even for a few weeks, but I knew Melissa was right.

"Do I need to ask . . ." I hesitated. I never know what to call Dessert Dad at work. "My father?" I finished.

Just as I said that, Marc Daniel Brown walked into the kitchen.

"Hey, Katie," he said. "Your mom asked if I could give you a ride home today. Are you ready now?"

"Oh, sure," I said. I started to take off my apron.

"Katie's going to need a few Saturdays off to get ready for her move," Melissa piped up, and I was grateful. "That's fine with me, if it's okay with you."

"Me? Yeah, that's fine," Dessert Dad said.

"Thanks, Melissa," I said.

"Let me know how everything goes," she said, and I nodded. Then I followed MDB out to the parking lot and got into his car.

I'd spent more time talking to Melissa than to him since I'd started working at the restaurant, so things were still kind of awkward whenever we were alone. We rode in silence for the first few blocks, and then Dessert Dad cleared his throat.

"So, um, your mom told me that the wedding is coming up soon. And also that you're moving into a new house," he said.

"Uh-huh," I replied.

"Are you, um, okay with all that?" he asked.

A few months ago, my reaction might have been to snap at him. *Why do you care? You haven't been a part of my life for years!* But my anger at MDB had cooled off a bit. And I could tell from the sound of his voice that he genuinely cared.

"It's fine," I said. "I mean, it's a lot of changes. And I'm a little freaked out about it. But I think it will be okay."

"Jeff seems nice," Dessert Dad said.

"He is," I agreed.

"Well, Jasmine and I," he began, (Jasmine is his wife), "we talked, and if you ever decided you wanted to come live with me and the girls, you'd be welcome to, Katie."

My jaw *literally* dropped, if that means that my mouth fell open and I didn't close it for a good three minutes. Never in a million years did I expect Dessert Dad to ask me to come live with him. I realized right then that I had no desire to—even if I had to share a room with Emily, I knew I wanted to live with Mom and Jeff. But still . . .

"That's nice of you," I said. "I think I'm going to be all right with Mom and Jeff and Emily. But, you know, if that changes . . ."

"You're always welcome to live with us, Katie," he said. "Or even just spend a weekend once in a while. But that's up to you."

"Thanks," I said, and I meant it. I was relieved

that MDB wasn't insisting that I stay with him or demanding court-ordered visits. He was being totally cool about everything. I remembered I had fun with his daughters.

"Maybe we can do something with the girls again sometime. We haven't done that in a while," I said.

He smiled. "That would be nice."

"But when the wedding and everything's over," I said quickly.

"Of course!" MDB said.

He pulled up in front of my house, and we both got out of the car and did an awkward hug. Then I sprinted inside.

I found Mom and Alexis in the front hallway. The contents of our coat closet were strewn on the floor, and the living room was filled with empty boxes. Mom's short hair was tucked into a bandana, and her cheeks were flushed red.

"Alexis! You came early," I said.

"I wanted to get started," she explained. She had her curly hair pulled into a ponytail on top of her head. She pointed to the kitchen. "I made you a chart with stickies, one sticky for every area in the house that needs to get sorted and packed. Every desk and dresser, every closet, every space. It helps keep packing focused, and you can tackle one small thing at a time. Your mom decided to start with this hall closet."

"We have so many umbrellas!" Mom said. She looked freaked out. "How did we end up with so many umbrellas?"

"Like I told you, Mrs. B, keep two, and put the rest in the giveaway box," Alexis said.

"But which ones do I keep?" Mom asked. She held up a tiny one with yellow ducks on the umbrella part. "This was Katie's when she was a little girl! I can't get rid of it!"

Mom bit her lip, which she does when she's stressed out. I grabbed Alexis by the arm. "Come on. Let's start on my room. Mom, why don't you order the pizza?"

Mom nodded. "Pizza. I can do that."

Alexis and I marched up to my room, where she had already set up boxes and one big garbage bag.

"I think we should start with your clothes first, Katie," she said. "Of course, you'll need to keep your summer clothes in your dresser to get through the next few weeks. And your underwear and socks, stuff like that. But we can pack the fall and winter stuff, and we can also see what you might want to get rid of."

"Okay," I said. I pulled open my bottom dresser drawer, which was stuffed with sweaters. I stared at it. "How do I decide what to keep?"

"Well, there's a rule that if you haven't worn something in a year, you should give it away," Alexis said. "And did you see that show with Marie Kondo, that woman from Japan?"

I shook my head. "Why? Does she bake stuff?"

"No, she organizes things," Alexis said, and her eyes started to shine. "She's amazing! She says you should hold an object in your hand and ask if it brings you joy. If it doesn't, give it away or toss it out."

"Hmm," I said. I pulled an olive-green sweater that Grandma Carole had given me last Christmas out of the drawer. I had never worn it, even though it was comfy. I just think that olive green is such a depressing color. "No joy."

"Excellent!" Alexis said. She pointed to a box. "That's the giveaway box."

Going through the sweater drawer with Alexis was kind of fun. We got through the whole dresser pretty quickly.

"This is going much more smoothly than I imagined, Katie," Alexis said. "Now let's tackle the closet."

She opened the closet door—and an avalanche of stuffed animals fell on her.

"You've got to be kidding me!" she yelled, but she was laughing. "Katie, don't you keep clothes in here?"

"I do," I replied. "They're behind the stuffed animals."

Alexis looked around the room. Since I was a baby, I'd kept every stuffed animal ever given to me. Every animal I'd ever won on the boardwalk at the Jersey Shore. Every stuffed animal I'd bought with my allowance. They took up space on my bookshelves, they hung out in a hammock in the corner of the wall, and my favorite ones lived on my bed.

"Here's what we're going to do," Alexis said. "Let's put all the stuffed animals on your bed. Every single one. Then you're going to go through them one at a time."

"Got it!" I said.

I picked up a tiny pink rabbit that Mom had gotten for me on a trip to Pennsylvania.

"Joy," I said, and I put it in a fresh new box. Alexis wrote STUFFED ANIMALS on it.

Next I picked up a purple octopus with really cool googly eyes. "Mr. Wiggles!" I cried happily. "Joy!"

Next came a white teddy bear with a candy cane–striped scarf. A squirrel holding a nut. A black cat with green eyes.

"Joy! Joy! Joy!" I cheered, and I started throwing stuffed animal after stuffed animal into the box. "This is easy."

"Slow down, Katie!" Alexis said. "Take a breath. Do you *really* want to bring all these stuffed animals into your new bedroom?"

I looked at the huge pile of stuffed cuteness on my bed. "Well, I don't know," I said. "My new room will be a lot bigger. And these all bring me joy."

"Maybe they could bring somebody else joy," Alexis said. "Imagine a little kid getting this sweet stuffed snake as a gift."

"Not Sammy!" I cried, grabbing it from her, and she narrowed her eyes. I sighed.

"But maybe . . . this one," I said, picking up a brown teddy bear that I honestly couldn't remember where I got it.

"Good start," Alexis said.

I slowed down and plowed through the pile. That Marie lady was onto something. If I really thought about it, not *all* my stuffed animals made me feel joy. But most of them did.

Still, I had a nice pile going in the giveaway

box when Mom called to say the pizza had arrived. Alexis and I bounded down the stairs.

"Really nice job, Mrs. B," Alexis said. Mom had managed to sort through all the closet contents, and the floor was clear.

"You're right, Alexis. It's not bad if you just take it one step at a time," Mom said with a smile, and she looked relieved.

We went into the kitchen, where Alexis's chart waited for us on the table. The big sheet of poster paper was covered in sticky notes. Covered! There must have been a hundred. And they were all different colors.

"I used a different color for each room," Alexis said. "Katie, your room is pink. Go ahead, you can take off the dresser sticky note."

I found the note and took it off. It left a square-shaped hole on the board.

"That feels pretty good," I said.

Mom located the hall closet sticky note, took it off, and crumpled it up. "Done!" she said.

"Two down," I said. "And seventeen hundred to go."

Alexis rolled her eyes at me. "Oh, come on! It's not that many," Alexis said. "And after pizza, we can finish your closet, now that we can finally see the clothes. I cannot believe how much stuff you had in there."

"If you don't mind, Alexis, I need to do something with Katie this afternoon, before it gets too dark," Mom said. "But I am so grateful for all your help today. Please add the hours to your invoice."

"Oh, today was on me," Alexis said. "Packing and organizing is fun! And not as stressful as planning a wedding."

"If you say so," Mom said. "Thank you."

We wolfed down our pizza and cleaned up. Then Mom and I gave Alexis a ride home.

❀

"So what did you want to do with me?" I asked, after Alexis got out of the car. "Another surprise dance lesson with Donny?"

Mom smiled. "Nope. I wanted to give you a tour of the house. Just you and me."

"Cool," I replied, although I wasn't sure how cool I felt inside. The house had looked great in pictures, but what if it was creepy in person? Or smelled bad? Or was crawling with spiders?

My imagination was going full force as we pulled up to the yellow house on Willow Brook Road. The FOR SALE sign had a big SOLD banner stuck over it.

We walked up the steps and stopped on the porch. I turned around and looked at the park, and now my imagination had me sitting in a rocking chair, sipping lemonade, and watching the trees in the park blowing in the breeze.

"Can we get rocking chairs?" I blurted out.

Mom smiled as she opened the door. "Jeff and I were just talking about that."

We stepped into a small hallway, which had a big staircase heading upstairs right in front. To the left was a big room that I guessed was the living room, and to the right was a smaller room.

"That's going to be the dining room," Mom explained. "We won't have to eat in the kitchen all the time. So we can cook and leave a mess and then bring everything out onto a nice, empty table."

"The kitchen!" I cried, and I ran through the dining room into the kitchen. It was bigger than the one we had, and it had an island in it, just like I'd seen in the picture. I started opening up the white cabinets.

"Lots of storage space," I said. "It's cute!"

The window over the sink looked out into the backyard, a small, green space with a border of tall pine trees in the back.

"There's room for a vegetable garden, I think,"

Mom said. "Although it might be too shady with the trees."

By then I was dying to see my room, so I ran up the stairs two at a time. I ran into two rooms before I found the one from the picture.

"This is it, right?" I asked, as Mom caught up to me.

"Yes, this is yours," Mom said.

I looked around at the wood floor and the white walls. I opened up the closet, which was about the same size as the one I already had. But the room had something I hadn't noticed in the photo. A weird little nook in one corner, almost like a big closet without a door.

"This is cool," I said, stepping into it.

"It's a little bit odd," Mom admitted. "I think because this room was built around the staircase. I'm glad you don't mind it."

"No way!" I said. "It's like a secret space. Maybe I can make it into a reading corner, with a beanbag chair."

"I like that idea," Mom said. "We'd just have to make sure it was well lit."

I started to feel excited. This house was nice and new to me! Moving in would be like a fresh start. I began to imagine hanging out with my friends in the room and reading in my nook and playing music.

Mom showed me the rest of the rooms, and then we sat down on the steps outside.

"Jeff had an idea, and I think it's a good one," she began, and I laughed.

"Oh boy," I said. "All your ideas lately involve a lot of work."

"This one does too, but hear me out," Mom said. "Instead of the four of us moving into the house after the wedding, you and I could move in a couple of weeks before the wedding. I know there have been big changes, and everything has been happening quickly, so it's up to you. But Jeff said it might be nice for us to 'make ourselves at home' first before he and Emily move in. What do you think?"

At first I thought about how much we had left to pack.

"There are so many sticky notes," I said.

"I know, but I'm thinking we'll have two more weekends before the moving date," she replied. "And Mia's mom and Eddie offered to help."

"Emma offered to help me paint my new room before we moved in," I remembered.

"I think that could happen," Mom said. "And

your schoolwork. And planning for the wedding. Oh wow, now that I say it out loud . . ."

"No, we can do it!" I said. I really liked the idea of moving in early with just her. I imagined cooking breakfast for dinner in our beautiful new kitchen and eating in the dining area. I pictured the two of us sitting in rocking chairs on the porch, sipping lemonade and telling stories and laughing. The more I imagined it the more excited I became. "Let's try, anyway."

"Okay," Mom said, and she hugged me. "Should we go grab dinner at the diner?"

"Let's just eat leftover pizza," I said. "I want to rip off at least one more sticky note tonight!"

Mom grinned. "Alexis would be so proud of you right now."

CHAPTER 9

So Much Joy!

The next two weeks were the busiest weeks of my life. Mom had one rule for me: schoolwork before packing. Luckily, it was the end of the school year and homework was winding down, so I mostly just had to study for my final tests.

Every day after studying, I packed something. Every morning, Mom left the house with boxes or bags to drop off at the church thrift shop near her work. Then we counted the days till the weekend.

On the last Sunday before moving weekend, Emma and Mia had a surprise for me. Mia's stepdad, Eddie, drove us all to the new house and announced that we were going to be painting my new room.

"No way!" I cried, jumping out of the car. Eddie opened the trunk and revealed two cans of paint, some tarps, brushes, and bucket. Eddie took painting seriously.

"Yes way," Eddie said. "I patched up some of the nail holes in the walls last night, so we should be ready to go. We can knock it out this morning." He held out a can of paint. "Here, carry this," he said. "But don't spill it. I hear it's not easy being green."

Mia groaned, but Emma and I laughed. Eddie is the king of corny dad jokes. I didn't mind them, but Emma and I don't have to hear them all the time like Mia does.

Emma and I had picked out the paint colors over lunch during the week. At first I wanted to paint each wall a different color, but Emma had suggested that I just paint the little nook a separate color, and I liked that idea. I picked a sky blue for the walls to remind me of being outside, and a peaceful green for the nook.

Once we got to the room, we spread out the tarps to protect the floor, and Eddie poured the paint into trays. He dipped the roller into the tray and showed us how to apply the paint first in a W on the wall, and then fill in the W with paint. I thought it was strange at first, but then he showed me some videos on the Internet. Apparently a lot of people paint this way. It prevents drips or something like that.

Emma, Mia, and I each took a wall, and Eddie took the nook because he said it was tricky. I was amazed how quickly the room transformed from a nice, but kind of cold, white space into something really beautiful.

"So are you ready for the move?" Eddie asked from inside the nook.

"I don't know," I said. "We still have nine sticky notes left."

"That doesn't sound like a lot to pack," Eddie said.

"She's talking about the sticky notes that Alexis made for them," Mia joined in. "Each one is a different place they need to pack."

"Right," I said. "And the last nine are hard. One of them is the attic, which we haven't even touched yet! I don't know how we're going to get everything done by Saturday, when the movers come. But Mom's taking off from work starting tomorrow, so that should help."

"We'll be there Saturday to do whatever you need," Mia said.

"Are you sure?" I asked. "Doesn't Cupcake Club have an order that day?"

"Just two dozen cupcakes, and we can do that Friday night without you, Katie," Emma said, and she stopped me with her hand before I could protest. "This is a special time. We got this. You've always pitched in when I've been modeling."

"And when I'm at my dad's," Mia added.

I took a deep breath. "I guess you're right," I said. "Thanks."

We finished quickly, and I felt really happy. My new room was ready to move into!

Now I just had to finish packing. . . .

❧

"Who wants Chinese food?"

Jeff came into the house without knocking, holding two paper take-out bags.

"Hey, sweetie," Mom said, and she kissed him. "This is great. Did you get utensils? Because the kitchen is all packed up."

"Paper plates, napkins, forks, and chopsticks," Jeff reported, and he set it all out on the kitchen table.

I glanced at the clock. It was eight thirty, and Mom and I had been trying to finish packing before the move in the morning. We'd totally forgotten about dinner!

"I am so glad this isn't pizza," I said. "And I can't

believe I'm saying that. Thanks so much, Jeff!"

Mom and I were so hungry that we didn't say a word as we scarfed down our lo mein and egg rolls.

"I'll stay and help you pack," Jeff offered.

"We're almost done, and I think I'll drop if I pack another box," Mom said. "But thanks. Besides, you're coming here bright and early, aren't you?"

Jeff nodded. "I'll be here before the furniture truck gets here at seven thirty."

"Seven thirty?" I groaned. "Why so early? I'm going to need some coffee."

"I was planning to bring some for all of us," Jeff said.

"Mostly milk in Katie's coffee, please," Mom said. "But a little caffeine won't hurt any of us tomorrow, I'm guessing."

Mom's phone rang. "It's the caterer," she said. "Just give me a minute."

Mom walked into the dining room, and Jeff and I began to clean up. Jeff looked at me and suddenly broke out in a huge grin.

"You know, Katie, I just want you to know how happy I will be to be your stepdad," he said. "I'm excited that we're going to get to spend more time together, as a family, and I know Emily is thrilled to have a big sister."

I blushed. I think I was more nervous than excited, but Jeff was being so sweet. "Thanks," I said. "That's really nice."

Mom walked over to us and put the phone down. "Remind me again why we're moving and planning a wedding at the same time?"

Jeff got up and kissed her. "Because it's worth it," he said, and she looked into his eyes and smiled. He turned to me. "Bye, Katie." Then he left the house, humming.

"How are we doing with sticky notes?" I asked Mom.

She moved aside some boxes to find the chart. "One left!" she said. "There's still some stuff in the attic. But we can finish that in the morning. It doesn't need to be sorted. We can just throw it in boxes."

I nodded. "Sounds good to me," I said, yawning. "I'm going to crash."

"Before you do . . . ," Mom said, and she walked over to her bag. She took out two envelopes and handed them to me.

"Two envelopes? What are these? Cold hard cash?" I joked.

"These are for you to read on the wedding day, Katie," Mom told me.

"More surprises?" I asked.

"Not surprises," Mom promised.

I wasn't sure if I believed her, but I packed the envelopes in my backpack and then headed upstairs to spend the last night in my bedroom. Every last sock, stuffed animal, and book was packed. Mom had set out a pillow and sleeping bag on my bed for me to sleep in because my sheets and blankets were packed.

After I got into pj's, I turned out the light and snuggled into my sleeping bag. As my eyes adjusted to the darkness, I gazed up at the patterns on the ceiling and the peeling wallpaper. I would always love this room and this house, but slowly and surely, the idea of leaving it was starting to hurt less and less. I was ready for a new home and a new adventure.

"Thanks for being a good bedroom," I said out loud. "You brought me joy."

Then I thought of the new sky-blue walls waiting for me, and I smiled. I felt better knowing those walls would bring me joy too.

❁

I woke up at seven and quickly got dressed and rolled up my sleeping bag. Then I ran downstairs to find Jeff in the kitchen.

"Good morning, Katie," Jeff said. He handed me a paper cup with a lid on it. "Mocha for you, mostly milk."

"Yes!" I said, and I took the cup from him. Then I noticed the pink box on the kitchen table. "Are those doughnuts?"

"Breakfast of champions," Jeff joked, and I grabbed a chocolate-glazed one to go with my mocha. Then Mom came into the kitchen and kissed Jeff.

"Okay, we are almost ready," she said. "When are the movers getting here?"

Before Jeff could answer, we heard the groan of the loud truck outside.

"I think they're here," he said.

"They can't be!" Mom said. "I don't have all the boxes ready yet."

"André, Bill, and I are getting the boxes this afternoon," Jeff reminded her. "These guys are just getting the big furniture."

"Of course!" Mom said. "I have never been this scatterbrained in my whole life."

"You have never had this much going on at once in your whole life," Jeff said kindly.

"Deep breaths, Mom," I said, with a mouthful of doughnut.

"Katie, can you finish the attic on your own?" Mom asked.

"Got it," I said, and then three really big guys in blue coveralls walked into the house, so I grabbed some boxes and slipped away upstairs. Everything was going according to plan.

Most of the stuff in the attic was already in cardboard boxes, so I started carrying those downstairs. On my third trip down, Alexis and Emma walked in the front door.

"We're here to help!" Emma said.

"And we brought cupcakes!" Alexis thrust out a cupcake carrier. I took it from her and peeked under the lid. The cupcakes had blue icing, like my room, with a little fondant house on top of each one.

"So cute!" I said. "I'll put these in the kitchen, next to the doughnuts. I bet the movers will like them, too."

Then Alexis and Emma followed me upstairs.

"You know Mia's with her dad, or she would be here," Emma said. "Plus, she says she's working all weekend to finish your dress."

"I totally forgot about that," I admitted. "Alexis, how is everything coming along for the wedding, anyway?"

"Jeff got the park permit, the catering menu has been set, and I just got the song requests to the deejay," she reported. "The flowers have been ordered, and I got your mom to hire Adele's Chocolates to do the favors. There's not much left to do. Those e-mail invitations saved us a lot of time."

"Great," I said. "Now I just need to get some help moving these boxes, if you guys don't mind doing this with me."

"No problem," Alexis said. "What are these? Photo albums?"

She picked one up and began to leaf through it.

"I think so," I said.

Emma looked over Alexis's shoulder. "Oh, look! It's tiny Katie!"

"Let me see," I said, and Alexis passed the album over to me. There was a picture of me in first grade, with my best friend Callie and three other girls from my class. We were sitting around my kitchen table, and I was about to blow out candles on a birthday cake with chocolate frosting.

"Oh wow," I said, "I forgot about that party." I looked through the album. There was me running under the sprinkler in the front yard. And me opening presents under the Christmas tree. And me sitting on Grandma Carole's lap in the rocking chair in the living room. So many, many memories! How could I ever leave this place?

And then, just like that, I wasn't fine with it anymore. My eyes filled with tears again. "I'm going to miss this house," I sobbed. "I love the new house and my new room and everything, but this house has been my whole life. I have so many memories here!"

"Just think of all the new memories you'll make in the new house," Alexis said.

"Right," Emma agreed. "And you'll be making them with a whole new family. A family that tiny Katie never thought she would have."

"Emma, that's so deep," I said, and I did that thing where you're crying but you laugh and it sounds like a hiccup. "You guys need to be part of those memories. You both and Mia!"

Then I started crying again. "This is terrible! How can I be happy and sad at the same time?"

Alexis pulled me up from the floor. "Calm down, Katie," she said. "I know what you need. Let's bring some of these boxes downstairs."

We each carried a box down from the attic and sat at the kitchen table. Alexis opened the carrier and handed me a cupcake.

"Take a deep breath. Then take a bite," Emma instructed, and I obeyed. The sweetness of the cupcake immediately made me feel a little better.

"Ah," I said. "The cupcake cure. See? I'm not crying."

"Those claims are not verified by the FDA," Alexis joked. "But I'm pretty sure you're right."

Mom came into the kitchen. "Hi, girls! Katie, that kitchen table is being loaded up next."

The three of us jumped up and moved the cupcakes and the doughnuts onto the counter. Then we went back up to the attic and finished packing. I avoided looking at the photo albums this time. We needed to say focused!

After the furniture truck was packed, Jeff followed them to the new house, and Jeff's friends André and Bill came by with a small-box truck. Emma and Alexis stayed to help us move boxes from the house to the truck, and Bill stacked them on to it. After the box truck was filled, we filled Bill's pickup truck and Mom's trunk.

"Katie, check the house. Did we get everything?" Mom asked.

I jogged through every room of the house, silently thanking each one. When I finished, I picked up my backpack, and Alexis and Emma grabbed whatever cupcakes were left. I locked the door behind me, and we piled into Mom's car.

It was only a fifteen-minute drive to the new house, and the furniture guys were already busy moving stuff in. Then André and Bill got to work unloading the boxes with Jeff. Alexis and Emma helped, and then we all took a break when Alexis's mom brought over some sub sandwiches at lunchtime. Apparently she'd heard that we were pizza'd out.

"Katie, your furniture is set up in your room, and I think most of your boxes are up there," Jeff said. "Why don't you, Alexis, and Emma start setting things up the way you want them?"

"Sounds good to me," I agreed, and the three of us made our way up there.

The room already looked different with my dresser, desk, bookshelf, and bed in place. The first thing I did was open the bag with my sheets, pillows, and bedspread, and we set up the bed. Then I flopped down on it.

"I'm done!" I announced, and Emma joined me. Alexis picked up a box marked STUFFED ANIMALS.

"Honestly, Katie, where are you going to put all these?" Alexis asked.

"Put them on me," I said. "They bring me joy!"

"What do you mean?" Alexis asked.

"PUT THEM ON ME!" I said loudly, collapsing into giggles.

Emma jumped up and tore open the box. Then she and Alexis dumped all the stuffed animals on top of me.

"So much joy!" I cried, and soon we were all cracking up hysterically.

Mom appeared in the doorway. She took in the three of us howling with laughter and me covered in stuffed animals. "All right, you three are clearly exhausted. Let's call it a day! Alexis and Emma, thank you so much for your hard work today. Is it okay if I drive you home?"

"No problem, Mrs. B," Alexis said. "I've got to go work on your seating chart."

Mom shook her head. "I don't know how you do it, Alexis," she said. "Katie, I'll be right back."

I hugged my friends good-bye, and then I climbed back onto the bed with the stuffed animals. I chilled out and listened as the guys carried stuff through the house. After a while I got up and tried to unpack a box, but I gave up. I walked back downstairs and helped Jeff and his friends move boxes.

✿

It only took a couple more hours to get everything into the house. Mom, Jeff, and I ate the leftover subs, and then Mom and Jeff talked on the porch for a little while. Later, Mom came in and sat down next to me.

"Same table, different house," she said. "What do you think, Katie?"

"I think we have a lot of unpacking to do," I said, and she ruffled my hair.

"You've been working so hard, and I'm so grateful to you," she said. "Don't worry. I have off again this week, and I'll get a lot put away while you're at school. And Mia's mom is coming to help tomorrow."

I stood up and stretched. "I think I need to go to sleep."

"I'll walk you up," Mom said, and she waited while I got into pj's and brushed my teeth, and then she tucked me into bed, piling more stuffed animals on top of me while I laughed.

"Are you going to be okay?" she asked.

"I think so," I said. "Love you, Mom."

"Love you, too, Katie," she replied.

I took one long look around the room. *My first night in my new room in my new home,* I thought. And I didn't feel the least bit sad. I was fine again.

I imagined it might be this way for a little while, with happiness and homesickness coming in waves.

Then I curled up with my stuffed animals and fell into a deep sleep.

CHAPTER 10

I Have a Date for the Wedding!

When I stepped on the bus Monday morning, it was about half as full as usual. That's because I got on the bus earlier now, which meant I had to wake up earlier from now on. But it meant more time with Mia, so it all evened out.

"Katie!" Mia cried happily when she saw me. "How'd it go? I wanted to stay here and help, but Dad is letting me stay in Maple Grove already for the wedding, and . . ."

"It's fine," I assured her. "Emma said you were busy working on my dress, anyway."

Mia smiled. "Oh, Katie, you're going to love it! I've still got a lot to do, but I know I'll get it finished in time. I'm going to spend all this weekend working on it. I'm in design mode!"

I nodded. "Now that the move is over, we're in wedding mode from now on. There's a ton of stuff to unpack, but we're not sweating it. Plus, your mom came over and helped my mom unpack the kitchen, and that's the most important room in the house, anyway."

"Mom was saying that we should bake the wedding cupcakes at our house, the day before the wedding," Mia said. "To give you guys a break."

"That's probably smart," I said. "Mom's pretty calm now, but who knows what she'll be like right before the wedding?"

The bus stopped, and George got on. He strolled down the aisle and sat in the empty seat behind me and Mia. I realized then that I had never asked him to the wedding to help with the cupcakes. Mia gave me a look, and I leaned over the seat to talk to him.

"Hey, you're back in your seat," I said. George hadn't sat behind us since that day Ken was sick.

"Hey, you're on the bus early," he said.

"Yeah, I moved," I told him.

His eyes got wide. "So fast? I thought you were busy with the wedding?"

"I was—am," I said. "But Mom and Jeff bought a house, and then Mom had this idea that we should move in early. So we did this weekend."

"Wow, moving's not easy," he said. "Where are you living now?"

"By the park," I told him. Then I changed the subject and asked him something I'd been afraid to ask. "Are we cool? I feel like you've been avoiding me lately."

George looked surprised. "Of course we're cool," he replied. "I just figured you were busy with the wedding and you needed some space. You've seemed kind of stressed lately, and you were too busy to hang out. But I get it. You've got a lot going on right now."

I laughed. "I thought *you* were the one who needed some space from me."

George laughed too. "I guess from now on we should talk about stuff. I mean, that's what friends do, right?"

"Right," I said, and I felt my cheeks getting warm. George is a friend, yeah, but I also feel as though I like *like* him sometimes, which is nice— but can be confusing.

"So, I was wondering if you would be able to help us with the cupcakes at the wedding," I said. "Not, like, working the whole time because you could, you know, eat and—" George wouldn't even let me finish the sentence.

"I'd love to come!" he said. "I'll do whatever you need. And if I get a break, I'll bust some moves on the dance floor for you."

"I don't know if you'll be able to keep up with me," I told him. "I have had a professional lesson. I can move from side to side and swing my arms."

"Did you say 'swing my arms'? You'd better be careful on the dance floor, Katie," George teased. "You might give somebody a black eye!"

I shook my head and turned back in my seat, but I was smiling. Mia squeezed my hand and nodded approvingly at me. I pictured myself dancing with George in my beautiful new dress. For the first time, I started thinking about how fun the wedding was going to be!

❖

Once the move was over, everything became eerily calm for Mom and me. Because we were right across from the park, she and I were able to run together every morning. It was a great way to work off wedding anxiety, and I got to spend extra time with Mom too.

The last few days of school were busy with exams at first, and then when exams were over, we did things like watch movies in class. Homework stopped, and at night Mom and I slowly worked on getting the house ready for Jeff and Emily. Jeff came over one night to paint Emily's room pale pink, and I helped. He was pretty impressed with my *W* technique.

❧

Finally, it was the day before the wedding. Grandma Carole and Grandpa Chuck showed up at the new house that Friday afternoon.

"Grandma! Grandpa!" I cried, and I raced down the steps for a group hug. Grandma Carole looked up at the house.

"Well, this is just lovely," she said. "Do you like it, Katie?"

"I love it," I told her. "Come on. Let me show you my room!"

Before we could get to my room, we ran into Mom, and there was a lot of hugging and crying and stuff. Especially my mom and grandma. They just looked at each other and got weepy and hugged for a really long time.

"You know, I never even asked where you were going to stay," Mom told her parents. "Do you want to take Katie's room?"

"We booked a hotel room in Stonebrook," Grandpa Chuck replied. "We figured the house might not be ready for guests."

"And I reached out to Jeff's mom on Facebook," Grandma Carole said. "We've got dinner reservations tonight at seven for all of us. I know you didn't want a rehearsal dinner, but . . ."

Mom hugged Grandma Carole. "No, that's perfect. Thank you!" she said. "Have you checked in to your hotel yet?"

Grandma shook her head.

"Then maybe you could give Katie a ride to Mia's house on your way?" Mom asked. "She and her friends are baking the wedding cupcakes this afternoon."

"Wait until you see them," I promised my grandparents. "They're going to be amazing."

"Of course they are," Grandma Carole said. "You are an amazing baker!"

I showed Grandma and Grandpa my room, and they had lots of nice things to say about the paint job and my school grades and how beautiful I was going to be as a maid of honor. They are really great for my self-esteem!

✿

Then they dropped me off at Mia's. When I walked in, I could hear Dan and Sebastian playing guitar in the basement. Mia, Emma, and Alexis were already in the kitchen.

114

"Katie! Can you believe tomorrow is finally the big day?" Emma asked.

"It doesn't seem real," I admitted. "But I think I'm kind of excited. It's about time! Up until now I was just kind of nervous."

"Awesome, Katie!" Mia said.

"Okay, Cupcakers, we have ten dozen cupcakes to bake," Alexis said. "I'm thinking we should get the dozen gluten-free out of the way first, and make sure we label them and keep them separate."

"Sounds good," Mia said. Then she winked at Alexis and Emma. "First, I need to show Katie something."

Alexis and Emma smiled at each other, like they knew something I didn't. I quickly figured it out when Mia brought me up to her room. There, on a dress form, was my beautiful dress!

I gasped. It was even prettier than Mia's sketch. The pink color was more like a soft rose, the delicate cap sleeves looked dreamy, and there was a shiny satin sash around the waist in a deeper pink. "And look!" Mia said, and she lifted up the dress to show me the hem.

The very bottom of the dress had a tiny border, less than a half an inch thick. It was a sparkly, sheer, gossamer material that had all the colors of the rainbow! It added a tiny shimmer to the dress and made it look even more magical.

"I was almost finished with the dress," Mia said. "And then this shiny rainbow material caught my eye. And I thought 'I have to add a rainbow to Katie's dress! She always says rainbow is her favorite color!'"

My eyes filled with tears again, and this time they were only happy tears. "Mia, I can't believe you made this for me," I said. "You are so talented!"

"The best part about making it was making it for you," Mia said. "I can't wait to see you in it, Katie."

I hugged her. "Thank you sooooo much."

Mia left the room, and I tried on the dress. It fit perfectly. I called her back in, and we stood in front of the mirror together. I couldn't believe how awesome I looked! And I do not like wearing dresses.

"Maybe you could put your hair up," Mia said, pulling my hair into a bun with her hand.

"Joanne from Mom's office is doing our hair and makeup tomorrow morning," I said. "I'll see what she thinks."

I looked at myself in the mirror and sighed. "I don't want to take it off."

"Well, you'd better, unless you want to get frosting all over it," Mia said.

"I almost forgot why I came here!" I said. "We've got a hundred and twenty cupcakes to bake!"

CHAPTER 11

The Big Day

We baked, we frosted, and we decorated. We hadn't finished with all the cupcakes when Mom came with Grandma and Grandpa to go out to dinner.

"I should stay until we're done," I said.

Alexis gave me a shove. "You are done! From this point on, you only need to worry about the wedding. Now go!"

I knew she was right, but there was one thing I had to do. I hugged Alexis, Emma, and Mia one by one.

"You are the best friends ever," I said.

Mia brushed the flour off my jeans. "We love you, Katie. Now get out of here!"

I ran out to the car, and we went out to eat with Jeff and Emily and Jeff's parents, Leslie and James.

It was nice, but the restaurant was loud and there was a lot of talking and I was soooo tired from all the cupcake baking. I was glad when Grandma and Grandpa finally dropped Mom and me off at the house.

❀

My phone alarm woke me up at seven. The wedding day was finally here! I went downstairs and found Mom in sweats and a T-shirt, drinking coffee. She looked relieved to see me. She was a little paler than usual.

"You're up early," she said.

"It's the big day!" I said. "Are you nervous?"

"Very," Mom replied. "Want to go for a run?"

I grinned. A few minutes later Mom and I were on the trail. The sky was blue and a cool breeze was blowing. We did our usual route, which takes about thirty minutes, but before we got to the house, we stopped in front of the lake and sat on a bench.

"Katie, I just want to say how proud I am of you for how mature you've been through this whole process," Mom said. "Thank you."

"I'm happy for you," I said. "That's the most important thing. I love you."

Mom hugged me. "I love you, too, Katie, more than the moon and the sun and the stars and the sky!" She was crying now. "No matter what happens today, tomorrow, or anytime in between, you are the most important thing in the world to me. You will always come first in my life."

Those were the exact words I needed to hear, and I took them in without saying anything. Mom and I walked back to the house. I remembered the two envelopes Mom gave me and said not to open until the wedding day.

"Mom, you said I should open those two envelopes today," I said. "Should I open them now?"

"That's a good idea," she replied. "Do you want to be alone?"

I shook my head. "No, stay with me."

I brought the envelopes to the kitchen, and we sat at the island. I opened up the first one and read.

Dear Katie,

The other day I didn't say everything I needed to say to you. First of all, I want you to know how happy I am for your mom and Jeff. Your mom is great and deserves a happy life.

Also, I just want you to know that I didn't do the right thing when I left you and your mom. That was wrong. I am sorry that I missed out on

*seeing you growing up. I am sorry that I wasn't
there when you needed me. But I promise that I
will always be here for you from now on. If you
ever need anything, just ask.*

*I love you, and I am very proud to have you as a
daughter.*

Dad

"Whoa," I said, and I handed the letter to Mom.
While she read it, I thought about how Marc Daniel
Brown had signed the letter.

Dad.

It didn't bother me so much, now that he'd really
and truly apologized. Maybe one day he could be
more of a dad and less of a Dessert Dad.

"You okay?" Mom asked.

I nodded. "Yeah," I said. "That was good."

Then I opened the next letter.

Dear Katie,

*It really means a lot to me that you have
accepted me and Emily in your life. I love you
and your mom so much, and I can't wait for the
Brown-Green clan to get rolling! I am so happy
and proud that we will now be family.*

*I promise to do my best to be a good stepdad,
and I will love you and take care of you forever.*

Love always,

Jeff

Jeff's letter reminded me of something. When he and mom got engaged, he gave me a little heart necklace. He gave one to me and one to Emily.

I gave Jeff's letter to Mom to read and said, "I have to get out the heart necklace Jeff gave me. I really want to wear it today." I suddenly realized that my cheeks were wet with tears. I hadn't even realized I was crying!

"All I do is cry these days," I said, reaching for a tissue.

"Me too," Mom said, and we both laughed.

"You know, when I was little I sometimes wished for a dad or imagined I had a big family," I said. "I guess now my wish has come true!"

Mom hugged me. "You deserve for all your wishes to come true," she said. "Come on. We should go shower before Joanne gets here to do our hair and makeup."

We walked upstairs, and I was shocked to find Mia in Mom's room. My maid of honor dress was hanging on the closet and so was a beautiful, short white wedding dress!

I looked at Mom, who was smiling. "Did you know about this?" I asked.

Mom nodded. "I had a dress from an event a few years ago, and I asked Mia's advice about it."

"I thought it might look nice with a little bit of lace added, and I brought the idea to my design teacher in Manhattan," Mia said. "She did a sketch, and your mom commissioned her to finish it."

I got a closer look at the dress. It had a slightly flared knee-length skirt, and was topped by lace on a scoop neckline that also covered the shoulders.

"I haven't had a chance to try it on yet," Mom said.

"That's why I'm here," Mia said. "On-the-spot alterations, if you need them."

We sprang into action. I showered and washed my hair. Mom tried on the dress, and it fit perfectly, so Mia went home to get changed. Then Joanne showed up, and Mom showered while Joanne worked on me.

"Mia thought my hair would look good swept up," I told her.

"I think that's a great idea," Joanne agreed. "First, let's do your face."

She opened up her makeup case and took out a palette of eye shadow. I panicked a little bit at the sight of all the greens, purples, and blues.

"I don't really want a lot of makeup," I said.

"And you don't need it," Joanne said. She put some light brown mascara on my eyelashes, blended some pale pink onto my cheeks, and finished with pink lip gloss. Then she tucked the lip gloss into a little white beaded bag on a chain and handed it to me.

"For touch-ups," she said.

Then she did my hair, sweeping it up into a bun. But when she was finished I frowned.

"What's the matter?" Joanne said.

"It does look pretty," I told her. "But it doesn't look like me. And also I'm going to dance a lot, and I want my hair to be free and swinging when I do."

Joanne smiled. "Down it is," she said. And she got rid of the bun and made my hair shiny in soft waves past my shoulders. I loved it! By that time, Mom was showered and it was her turn. Joanne used the same colors on her, and used a blow dryer to get her short hair sleek and shiny.

When she finished, Mom and I both looked into the big mirror above her dresser. For a second, I thought I was looking at two strangers. We looked great, and still like ourselves, but at the same time so different!

"What do you think?" Joanne asked.

Mom grinned. "I think that we are ready for a wedding!"

CHAPTER 12

Mr. and Mrs. Jeffrey Green

Joanne left, and Mom and I put on our dresses. I helped Mom zip up her dress, and she buttoned up mine. Then I slipped on the pale pink shoes with the tiny kitten heels that Mia had found for me online.

Grandma Carole and Grandpa Chuck came to take us to the park, and they started crying when they saw us. Then they drove us to the main park entrance, which is about five minutes away.

"How is this going to work?" Grandma Carole asked as we pulled into the parking lot. "The ceremony is in the middle of the park, right? But we can't just walk in there. Jeff shouldn't see you before the wedding. Nobody else should, either. You should make an entrance!"

I knew the park pretty well. The wedding was going to be held at the gazebo in the center of the park. There was a tree-lined path to the gazebo, and already we could see wedding guests making their way there.

"Alexis came up with a plan," I said. "Mom and I are going to take the path over by the kids' park to the gazebo and sort of hide out there until it's time for the wedding."

"You're going to hide?" Grandma asked.

"It'll be fine, Mom," my mom told her.

We all got out of the car, and Grandma Carole and Grandpa Chuck walked with us to the kids' park. I did feel a little silly when we got to the big clump of bushes and stopped. A lot of the little kids were pointing at us and staring.

"We'll go find our seats," Grandma Carole said, and she and Grandpa headed off.

Mom and I held hands and waited. It gave me a chance to get a good look at the setup. White folding chairs had been placed in front of the gazebo, and the aisle between them was lined with white and pink roses. Reverend Noll from Jeff's church stood in the gazebo, smiling and wearing gray robes and a pink flower tucked behind her ear. Jeff stood next to her, looking nervous in a black suit with a pink rose pinned to his jacket pocket. He looked nervous but handsome, too.

To the left of the gazebo, I was shocked to see Dan and Sebastian playing guitar. Usually, they were playing heavy metal music on electric guitars. But today they were both strumming pleasantly on acoustic guitars.

Soon all the chairs were filled, and Alexis came over to us with Emily. Emily looked cute in a simple pale pink dress that went well with her dark hair. She stood next to me, and her eyes were shining. I noticed she was wearing her heart necklace too.

"Wow, you all look so beautiful!" Alexis said.

"So do you," I told her, and I meant it. Alexis had tied her red curls in a pretty side ponytail, and she wore a yellow dress with white polka dots. Alexis looked at my mom. "Are you ready, Mrs. B?"

Mom took a deep breath and nodded. "Ready!"

We followed Alexis to the aisle, and everyone turned back to look at us. Then Alexis nodded to Dan and Sebastian, and they started playing the wedding march on their guitars. I thought it sounded really pretty that way.

"All right, Emily, you're going to walk down first," Alexis instructed. "When you get to the gazebo, take a seat in the front row."

Emily nodded and slowly walked down the aisle. Then Mom and I walked down the aisle, hand in hand, which is not what normally happens at a wedding but what Mom wanted.

My heart felt warm looking at the smiling faces staring at us. There was Emma with her mom and dad and her cute little brother, Jake. Emma looked adorable in a pale lavender dress that really made her blue eyes shine.

Alexis slid into a seat next to her mom and dad and her sister, Dylan. Then there was Mia, with her mom and Eddie. Mia had worked so hard to make my mom and me look gorgeous, and she looked beautiful in a sky-blue dress that I was pretty sure she'd made herself.

George had even come to the ceremony, and I noticed he'd dressed up in black dress pants and a white button-down shirt. He gave me a really big smile, pointed to my dress, and gave me a thumbs-up when I walked past.

I saw Jeff's parents and his best friends, and Joanne and Nina from Mom's work. A bunch of our teachers from our school were there too, which was weird but also amazing: It was like everyone in my life was at the wedding!

When we got to the gazebo, Mom squeezed my

hand and let it go. I sat down next to Emily, and she smiled at me.

Then Mom stepped onto the gazebo and faced Jeff. I had never seen him look so happy before, not even when he proposed to Mom and she said yes. They both had tears in their eyes, and I fought back my own.

Then I glanced at Emily, who was giggling nervously, and I joined her. A feeling washed over me. In that moment, I knew that everything was going to be all right because I had the best friends and the best new family that anyone could ask for.

CHAPTER 13

Change Is Beautiful

The reception took place immediately after the ceremony. We walked in and I let out a little gasp. The room looked like something out of a fairy tale! There were candles and clear vases filled with pink and white rosebuds on every table. Emma's favorite color in the world is pink, and she was swooning. "I want to *live* in this room!" she said.

"Katie, look!" Mia cried, pointing. In the far corner of the room stood our cupcake tower in all its glory.

I had left before it was completed, so this was my first real look at it. Every cupcake was iced with beautiful, delicate tiny roses. And . . . something else. "Are those . . . pearls?" I asked.

Mia nodded excitedly. "Edible pearls! I saw

them online and I couldn't resist. I wanted these cupcakes to be extra special."

And real roses surrounded the base of the tower, adding another "extra special" touch.

A couple of the wedding guests stopped by to take photos of the wedding cupcakes.

"Oh, it looks too pretty to eat!" one guest moaned.

"Oh no! After all the hard work we did baking those cupcakes, I want you to eat and enjoy every single bit of it," Alexis said.

"Do you mean to say you girls made these cupcakes?" the guest asked.

"We absolutely did," Alexis said. And before the woman could say anything else, Alexis whipped out a business card and said, "Here's our card for you. Party cupcakes are our specialty!"

I shook my head in wonder at Alexis. "You never miss a trick, do you? You're always ready to promote our cupcake business."

Alexis nodded seriously. "You know my family motto: Failing to plan is planning to fail! Which reminds me . . ." She took out a stack of our business cards and placed them in a neat pile next to the cupcake tower for people to take. I swear, Alexis could take over the world someday! She's that organized. I so admire that about her.

The deejay put on a soft, slow, romantic song, and my mom and Jeff started dancing. Usually I'm not that into mushy stuff (ordinarily I would look at Mia and roll my eyes), but this was different. I loved seeing my mom so happy. She was positively glowing, looking up at Jeff. And Jeff was beaming down at my mom.

"This is the best wedding I've ever been to in my life!" Emma sighed.

I grinned at her. "The romance is off the charts," I agreed. "You must be in your glory."

The song ended, and everyone applauded as my mom and Jeff kissed for what seemed like the millionth time that day.

Then I felt a tap on my shoulder. I spun around, and it was George! He had a big goofy grin on his face.

"Hi," he said.

"Hi," I answered back.

We were both quiet, and then we both giggled awkwardly.

"You clean up nice!" George finally said.

"So do you!" I answered.

Just at that moment, the deejay put on a lively tune.

"Are you ready to show me some moves, Silly Arms?" George asked.

I suddenly felt giddy.

"I am!" I said, and we started walking toward the dance floor.

And then I felt someone tugging at the back of my dress!

"Katie! Katie!" a familiar voice said.

I looked down, and it was Emma's little brother, Jake.

"Will you dance with me, Katie?" Jake asked.

"Oh, Jake, I'm just about to dance with George. I promise I will dance with you next," I said.

"Noooooooo! I. Want. To. Dance. With. You. NOWWW!" Jake yelled.

George laughed. "Hey, it's okay," he said. "We can dance—"

Just at that moment Mia glided over.

"You and Katie can dance right now," Mia said calmly. Just as Jake looked like he was about to let out another wail, Mia said, "Come on, Jake! You can dance with me. I've been dying to dance with you all day."

"You *have*?" Jake said with wide eyes.

"Oh, absolutely!" Mia replied. "And after you dance with me, I think Alexis has been waiting to dance with you too. And then after Alexis, you can dance with Katie."

"Wow! That sounds great!" Jake said. He grabbed Mia by the hand. "Come on. Let's dance right now!" He suddenly seemed to remember I was there. "See you later, Katie," he said. "Come on, Mia. Let's go!" he shouted.

Mia touched me lightly on the arm. "You owe me one," she said.

I laughed. "Don't I know it!" I said.

Once Jake was dancing (or rather, jumping up and down) with Mia, George and I walked out onto the dance floor. As soon as we were safely in a spot away from Mia and Jake, I twirled impulsively.

"Nice!" George said.

"It's the dress," I explained. "It makes me feel like twirling."

"Well, here, let me help you," George said. He took one of my hands, held it up high, and said, "Go ahead, twirl!" And I did.

Then George and I were both laughing and dancing to the beat. As I spun around and looked at all my family and friends in the room, I couldn't remember the last time I felt so happy. My heart was so full, I thought it might burst. *Cupcakes and wedding bells,* I thought. And change. Change is good. As long as you have friends and family who love you, I realized there was nothing to fear.

I hadn't noticed I had stopped dancing until I heard George say, "Don't stop now, Silly Arms, keep going!" I laughed and smiled and kept dancing with my friend. I wished the night could go on forever, but I knew whatever came after this would be great too! I was already looking forward to my next adventure.

Coco Simon always dreamed of opening a cupcake bakery but was afraid she would eat all of the profits. When she's not daydreaming about cupcakes, Coco edits children's books and has written close to one hundred books for children, tweens, and young adults, which is a lot less than the number of cupcakes she's eaten. Cupcake Diaries is the first time Coco has mixed her love of cupcakes with writing.

Here's a small taste
of the very first book in the

series written by Coco Simon:

Hole in the Middle

Donuts Are My Life

My grandmother started Donut Dreams, a little counter in my family's restaurant that sells her now-famous homemade donuts, when my dad was about my age. The name was inspired by my grandmother's dream to save enough money from the business to send him to any college he wanted, even if it was far away from our small town.

It worked. Well, it kind of worked. I mean, my grandmother's donuts are pretty legendary. Her counter is so successful that instead of only selling donuts in the morning, the shop is now open all day. Her donuts have even won all sorts of awards, and there are rumors that there's a cooking show on TV that might come film a segment about how she started Donut Dreams from virtually nothing.

My grandmother, whom I call Nans—short for Nana—raised enough money to send my dad to college out of state all the way in Chicago. But then he came back. I've heard Nans was happy about that, but I'm not because it means I'm stuck here in this small town.

So now it's my turn to come up with my own "donut dreams," because I am dreaming about going to college in a big, glamorous city somewhere far, far away. Dad jokes that if I do go to Chicago, I have to come back like he did.

No way, I thought to myself. Nobody ever moves here, and nobody ever seems to move away, either. It's just the same old, same old, every year: the Fall Fling, the Halloween Hoot Fair, Thanksgiving, Snowflake Festival, New Year's, Valentine's Day and the Sweetheart Ball . . . I mean, we know what's coming.

Everyone makes a big deal about the first day of school, but it's not like you're with new kids or anything. There's one elementary school, one middle school, and one high school.

Our grandparents used to go to a regional school,

which meant they were with kids from other towns in high school. But the school was about forty-five minutes away, and getting there and back was a big pain, so they eventually decided to keep everyone at the high school here. It's a big old building where my dad went to school, and his brother and my aunt, and just about everyone else's parents.

Some kids do go away for college. My BFF Casey's sister, Gabby, is one of them. She keeps telling Casey that she should go to the same college so they can live together while Gabby goes to medical school, which is her dream. It's a cool idea, but what's the point of moving away from everything if you just end up moving in with your sister?

Maybe it's that I don't have a sister, I have a brother, and living with him is messy. I mean that literally. Skylar is ten. He spits globs of toothpaste in the sink, his clothes are all over his room, and he drinks milk directly from the carton, which makes Nans shriek.

My grandparents basically live with us now, which is a whole long story. Well, the short story is that my mother died two years ago. After Mom died, everyone was a mess, so Nans and Grandpa ended up helping out a lot. Their house is only a short drive down the street from us, so it makes sense they're around all the time.

Even their dog comes over now, which is good because I love him, but weird because Mom would never let us get a pet. I still feel like she's going to come walking in the door one day and be really mad that there's a dog running around with muddy paws.

My mother was an artist. She was an art teacher in the middle school where I'm starting this year, which will be kind of weird.

There's a big mural that all her students painted on one wall of the school after she died. The last time I was in the school was when they had a ceremony and put a plaque next to it with her name on it. Now I'll see it every day.

It's not like I don't think about her every day anyway. Her studio is still set up downstairs. It's a small room off the kitchen with great light. For a while none of us went in there, or we'd just kind of tiptoe in and see if we could still smell her.

Lately we use it more. I like to go in and sit in her favorite chair and read. It's a cozy chair with lots of pillows you can kind of sink into, and I like to think it's her giving me a hug. Dad uses her big worktable to do paperwork. The only people who don't go in are Nans and Grandpa. Dad grumbles that it's the one room in the house that Nans hasn't invaded.

Sometimes I catch Nans in the doorway, though, just looking at Mom's paintings on the walls. Mom liked to paint pictures of us and flowers. One wall is covered in black-and-white sketches of us and the other is this really cool, colorful collection of painted flowers with some close up, some far away, and some in vases. I could stare at them for hours.

I remember there used to be fresh flowers all over the house. Mom even had little vases with flowers in the bathrooms, which was a little crazy, especially since Skylar always knocked them over and there would be puddles of water everywhere.

Sometimes when I had a bad day she'd make a special little arrangement for me and put it next to my bed. When she was sick, I used to go out to her garden and cut them and make little bouquets for her. I'd put them on her night table, just like she did for me. Nans always makes sure there are flowers on the kitchen table, but it's not really the same.

Grandpa and Nans own a restaurant called the Park View Table. Locals call it the Park for short.

DONUT DREAMS

They don't get any points for originality, because the restaurant is literally across from a park, so it has a park view. But it seems to be the place in town where everyone ends up.

On the weekends everyone stops by in the mornings, either to pick up donuts and coffee or for these giant pancakes that everyone loves. Lunch is busy during the week, with everyone on their lunch breaks and some older people who meet there regularly, and dinnertime is the slowest. I know all this because I basically grew up there.

Nans comes up with the menus and the specials, and she's always trying out new recipes with the chef. Or on us. Luckily, Nans is a great cook, but some of her "creative" dishes are a little too kooky to eat.

Nans still makes a lot of the donuts, but Dad does too, especially the creative ones. Donut Dreams used to have just the usual sugar or jelly-filled or chocolate, which were all delicious, but Dad started making PB&J donuts and banana crème donuts.

At first people laughed, but then they started to try them. Word of mouth made the donuts popular, and for a little while, people were confused because they didn't realize Donut Dreams was a counter inside the Park. They instead kept looking for a donut shop.

My uncle Charlie gives my dad a hard time sometimes, teasing him that he's the "big-city boy with the fancy ideas." Uncle Charlie loves my dad, and my dad loves him, but I sometimes wonder if Uncle Charlie and Aunt Melissa are a little mad that Dad got to go away to school and they went to the state school nearby.

My dad runs Donut Dreams. Uncle Charlie does all the ordering for food and napkins and everything you need in a restaurant, and Aunt Melissa is the accountant who manages all the financial stuff, like the payroll and paying all the bills. So between my dad, his brother, and his sister, and the cousins working at the restaurant, it's a lot of family, all the time.

My brother, Skylar, and I are the youngest of seven cousins. I like having cousins, but some of them think they can tell me what to do, and that's five extra people bossing me around.

"There's room for everyone in the Park!" Grandpa likes to say when he sees us all running around, but honestly, sometimes the Park feels pretty cro

That's the thing: in a small town, I alwa
there are too many people. Maybe it's ju

are too many people I know, or who know me.

Right after Mom died I couldn't go anywhere without someone coming up to me and putting an arm around me or patting me on the head. People were nice, don't get me wrong, but everyone knows everything in a small town. Sometimes I feel like I can't breathe.

Mom grew up outside of Chicago, and that's where my other grandmother, her mother, still lives. I call her Mimi. We go there every Thanksgiving, which I love. I remember asking her once when we were at the supermarket why there were so many people she didn't know. She laughed and explained that she lived in a big town, where most people don't know each other.

It fascinated me that she could walk into the supermarket and no one there would know where she had just been, or that she bought a store-bought cake and was going to tell everyone she baked it. No one was peering into her cart and asking what she was making for lunch, or how the tomatoes tasted last week. Nans always wonders if Mimi is lonely, since she lives by herself, but it sounds nice to me.

Everyone in our family pitches in, but I officially

start working at Donut Dreams next week for a full shift every day, which is kind of nice. I'll work for Dad. He bought me a T-shirt that says THE DREAM TEAM that I can wear when I'm behind the counter.

We have a couple of really small tables near the counter that are separate from the restaurant, so people can sit down and eat their donuts or have coffee. I'll have to clean those and make sure that the floor around them is swept too.

Uncle Charlie computerized the ordering systems last year, so all I'll have to do is just swipe what someone orders and it'll total it for me, keep track of the inventory, and even tell me how much change to give, which is good because Grandpa is a real stickler about that.

"A hundred pennies add up to a dollar!" he always yells when he finds random pennies on the floor or left on a table.

Dad will help me set up what we're calling my "Dream Account," which is a bank account where I'll deposit my paycheck. I figure if I can save really well for six years, I can have a good portion to put toward my dream college.

So we're going to the bank. And of course my

friend Lucy's mom works there. Because you can't go anywhere in this town without knowing someone.

"Well, hi, honey," she said. "Are you getting your own savings account? I'll bet you're saving all that summer money for new clothes!"

"Nope," said Dad. "This is college money."

"Oh, I see," she said, smiling. "In that case, let's make this official." She started typing information into the computer. "Okay. I have your address because I know it. . . ." She tapped the keyboard some more.

See what I mean? Everyone knows who I am and where I live. I wonder if people at the bank know how much money we have too.

After a few minutes, it was all set up. Afterward Dad showed me how to make a deposit and gave me my own bank card too.

I was so excited, not only because I had my own bank account, which felt very grown-up, but because the Dream Account was now crossed off my list, which meant I was that much closer to making my dream come true. I was almost hopping up and down in my seat in the car.

"You really want to get out of here, don't you?" asked Dad, and when he said it, it wasn't in his usual joking way. He sounded a little worried, and I immediately felt bad. It wasn't as if I just wanted to get away from Dad.

"You know," he said thoughtfully, "I get it."

"You do?" I asked.

"Yeah," he said. "I was the same way. I was itchy. I wanted to go see the big wide world."

We both stared ahead of us.

"I don't want to go to get away from you and Skylar," I said.

Dad nodded.

"But think of Wetsy Betsy."

Dad looked confused. "Who is Wetsy Betsy?"

"Wetsy Betsy is Elizabeth Ellis. In kindergarten she had an accident and wet her pants. And even now, like, seven years later, kids still call her Wetsy Betsy. It's like once you're known as something here, you can't shake it. You can't . . ." I trailed off.

"You can't reinvent yourself, you mean?" asked Dad.

"Exactly!" I said. "You are who you are and you can't ever change." I could tell Dad's mind was spinning.

"So who are you?" he asked after a few more minutes.

"What?" I asked.

"Who are you?" Dad asked. "If Elizabeth Ellis is Wetsy Betsy, then who are you?"

I took a deep breath. "I'm the girl whose mother died. I sometimes hear kids whisper about it when I walk by."

I saw Dad grimace. I looked out the window so I wouldn't have to watch him. We stayed quiet the rest of the way home.

We pulled up into our driveway and Dad turned off the car, but he didn't get out.

"I understand, honey. I really do. I understand dreaming. I understand getting away, starting fresh, starting over. But wherever you go, you take yourself with you, just remember that. You can start a new chapter and change things around, but sometimes you can't just rewrite the entire book," he said.

I thought about that. I didn't quite believe what he was saying, though. In school they were always nagging us about rewriting things.

"But you escaped," I said. "And then you just came back!"

"Well, you escape prison. I didn't see this place as a prison," Dad said. "But Nans as a warden, that's . . ."

He started laughing. "Seriously, though, I left because I wanted an adventure. I wanted to meet new people and see if I could make it in a place where everyone didn't care about me and where I was truly on my own. I never had any plans to come back, but that's how it worked out."

"So why did you move back here?" I asked.

"Because of Mom," said Dad. "She loved this place. I brought her here to meet everyone and she didn't want to leave."

"But Mimi didn't want her to move here," I said, trying to piece together what happened.

I had always thought it was Dad who wanted to move back home. Mom and Dad met in college. She lived at school like Dad did, but Mimi was close by, so she could drive over for dinner. Mom and Dad hung out at Mimi's house a lot while they were in college.

"Noooo," Dad said slowly. "Mimi wasn't too thrilled about Mom's plan. She didn't really understand why Mom would want to move out here, so far from her family, and especially where there weren't a lot of opportunities for artists."

"So she changed her mind?" I asked.

I never remembered Mimi saying anything bad

about where we lived, but Dad would always tease her, saying, "So it worked out okay, didn't it, Marla?"

She came to visit twice a year and always seemed to have a good time. "It's a beautiful place to live," she would say, smiling.

"Well," said Dad. "It took Mimi a while to change her mind. But she saw how happy Mom was and how much everyone here loved Mom, so she was happy that Mom was happy. That's the thing about parents. They really just want their kids to be happy, even if they don't understand why they do things. If you decide to move away from here, I'll miss you every day, but if that's what you want to do and that's what makes you happy, then I will be there with the moving truck."

"So if I tell you I want to move to Chicago for college, you'll be okay with that?" I asked.

"If you promise to come home and visit me a lot," said Dad, grinning.

"Deal!" I said.

"I love you," said Dad.

"I love you back," I said.

"Okay, kiddo, let's go in for dinner. Nans goes mad when we're late."

Hole in the Middle

"Dad, isn't it correct to say that Nans gets angry? Because, like, animals go mad but people get angry."

"In that definition, Lindsay, I think that is an entirely correct way to categorize your grandmother when you are late for dinner. She gets mad!"

I giggled and opened the car door.

"Ready, set, run to the warden!" said Dad, and we raced up to the house, bursting with laughter.